Readers love SJD PETERSON

Limitless

"I recommend this to everyone who's intrigued with BDSM, the Dom/sub relationship, the concept of pain mixed with pleasure, and flawed, realistic men who more than deserve a happy ending."

—Long and Short Reviews

"SJD Peterson def has a way of sucking in the readers. This book is the perfect example of that."

—Gay Book Reviews

Override

"I loved this story. Little angst, no anger issues, no overblown drama, just two men finding a way to meet in the middle and merge their worlds."

—Alpha Book Club

"The strength of *Override* is definitely the strong and steady connection between Seth and Donavan and their growing romance."

—Sinfully: Gay Romance Book Reviews

Bound

"SJD Peterson did a phenomenal job with this from beginning to end."

—Rainbow Gold Reviews

"If it all had to end then for me it ended perfectly."

—Prism Book Alliance

By SJD Peterson

Published by DREAMSPINNER PRESS
www.dreamspinnerpress.com

Something's Brewing at Joe's

SJD PETERSON

REAMSPINNER PRESS

Published by

DREAMSPINNER PRESS

5032 Capital Circle SW, Suite 2, PMB# 279, Tallahassee, FL 32305-7886 USA
www.dreamspinnerpress.com

Something's Brewing at Joe's
© 2017 SJD Peterson.

Cover Art
© 2017 Reese Dante.
http://www.reesedante.com
Cover content is for illustrative purposes only and any person depicted on the cover is a model.

ISBN: 978-1-63533-337-4
Digital ISBN: 978-1-63533-338-1
Library of Congress Control Number: 2016917541
Published June 2017
v. 1.0

Printed in the United States of America

This paper meets the requirements of
ANSI/NISO Z39.48-1992 (Permanence of Paper).

To LuLu, who tried her best to keep me
from writing this story. I win!

Chapter One

MURPHY COULD describe Florida in July in a single word—fuckinghot!

Okay, that was actually two words, but totally appropriate. He'd lived through some intense summer days back in Michigan, but the 100 percent humidity combined with ninety-plus temperature was something he could have lived without ever experiencing. Soaked in sweat, he slumped down on a park bench, wiped at his burning eyes, then slid his sunglasses back on to protect his retinas from being seared by the bright afternoon sun.

"What the hell am I supposed to do now?"

"Excuse me?"

Murphy snapped his head to the right. He'd been so lost in his thoughts he hadn't even noticed the elderly man sitting at the other end of the bench. "Sorry, was just thinking out loud."

The old man gave Murphy a disapproving look, grunted, then went back to reading his newspaper.

Murphy hung his head and ran his fingers through his sweat-soaked hair. Great, not only was there no job waiting for him, but the natives didn't seem to be all that friendly either.

Oh, what big plans he'd had. He was and always had been stubborn. Although that was what other people called him, Murphy wouldn't necessarily use that term to describe himself. It was more that he simply liked doing things his way. So he'd ignored the well-meant advice from friends and family, sold his truck, and bought an old Ford Focus. He'd also cleaned out his bank account, which hadn't been much—a whole nine hundred and forty-eight dollars—and hit the road. Probably should have thought about it a bit more thoroughly, but noooooo. Instead, he'd gotten a wild hair up his ass, and the next thing he'd known, he was on the road. Just jumped in with both feet and hoped he landed on them. Unfortunately, things hadn't gone as he'd planned. Now he was sitting on his ass in what felt like the bowels of hell.

While he might be a little impetuous, he wasn't a complete idiot. He'd left Michigan with the expectation of having a job when he arrived in Tampa. However, something about a protest, land rights, permits, blah, blah, blah—he'd stopped listening as panic zinged through him when they'd informed him the job was on hold until further notice. The bottom line was he was parked on a bench in the hot sun, ninety dollars less in his pocket, and no job.

Now he had two choices. Drive back to Michigan with his tail between his legs to a chorus of *I told you so* and beg for his old job back at the factory, or scan the local paper for work. Did he dare take a chance, spend money on a motel room, and hope he found a decent-paying job that would tide him over until when—if—the project resumed?

Choices, choices.

Mom and his siblings had called Murphy crazy. His friends told him he should wait. His recently-turned-ex–boyfriend Dylan had bet Murphy would return within two weeks, pleading with him to take him back. *Yeah, when hell freezes over.* Whether he returned to Michigan or not, Dylan would not be part of his future. The drama had been exhausting, and high-maintenance men were officially on his list of *never again*. Keeping men beyond a one-night stand was off the list as well. *From now on, it's all about me, me, me.* He'd learned his lesson. He was too young and had far too little patience to have to worry about someone's feelings full-time. Or whether he used the right cologne, shampoo, and wore matching shoes and belt, or wiped his feet and folded the bedspread back three-quarters of the way before getting in bed. Christ, just thinking about all the crap Dylan had nagged him about, it was surprising they'd lasted as long as they had—a full year and a half.

He pulled a cigarette from his shirt pocket, slid it between his lips, and fired up. He took a deep pull, the smoke burning his dry throat. The elderly man grunted again, waved a hand even though the wind was blowing the smoke away from him, and shuffled away. Murphy supposed he should be guilty for causing the old guy to leave, but he sort of felt vindicated after the man's rude attitude. Besides, the need for nicotine outweighed any discomfort or guilt, and he took another hit.

Resting his forearms on his denim-clad knees, he rolled the cigarette between his index finger and thumb, watching the smoke swirl upward and dissipate in the heavy air as he contemplated his current situation. Maybe his family was right, but going back seemed even more insane.

The thought of spending one more winter shoveling snow and scraping windshields made him feel physically ill.

Dammit, he was supposed to be starting his dream job in two days. He'd spent the last year busting his balls, working at night, going to trade school during the day to get his HVAR certificate. All the sacrifice had seemed worth it when the Barton Marlow Corporation offered him a job working in Florida. Okay, so it wasn't in his field—he'd be on the construction crew—but he'd have his foot in the door with one of the largest and most prestigious contracting companies in the state. It was a great opportunity to learn some new skills until something became available in heating and cooling.

Murphy took another long draw from his cigarette and held it in, letting the burn and the nicotine ground him as he considered his options. The only thing he got for his troubles was a dull ache in his temples. *Wait. Why am I putting all this pressure on myself?* He shook his head at his stupidity. He didn't need to decide at this very moment, and he damn sure didn't need to be making it after going without sleep for so long.

He finished his smoke and ground it out with the heel of his boot before pushing to his feet. He wasn't going to find any answers to his questions sitting in the sweltering sun. He could afford a cheap motel room for one night. Maybe after a cool shower, a couple of hours of sleep, and a decent meal, he'd grab a paper and check out the help-wanted ads. Tampa was a bustling town, and it was prime tourist season. Surely he could find something until BWC broke ground on the new condominium project.

Sitting in the driver's seat of his packed-to-the-gills car—sad that everything he owned fit in such a small space—Murphy started the car, then closed his hands around the steering wheel and instantly jerked them away.

"Ow! That's hot!" He shook his hands, as if it would actually help. He was going to melt. When he'd left home at the ass crack of dawn, he'd been dressed for the unseasonable cold snap that had made its way across the North and, in his hurry to get to Tampa, hadn't thought of changing. And just how damn stupid was that? His T-shirt clung to him; sweat trickled down his spine and temples, and he was pretty sure there was a full gallon of it in his boots. Worse, it ran from his brow into his eyes, burning them. He needed to find a room with a kickass air conditioner, and fast. He gritted his teeth, grabbed the wheel, and pulled onto the road. All his other concerns were trivial compared to his need to cool down before he ended up a crispy critter.

He didn't have far to drive before he spotted a Motel 6. The place was like an oasis: cheap, fairly clean, and air-conditioned. The instant Murphy was safely behind the locked door of his room, he removed his boots, peeled off his sweat-soaked clothes, and flopped onto the lumpy mattress with a sigh. The Tampa newspapers he'd picked up in the lobby would just have to wait a bit longer before he rummaged through the want ads. The excessive heat made him nauseous, and he was so tired his brain was fried, like deep Southern-fried. Sleep, all he needed was….

MURPHY JERKED awake and, for a few panic-filled seconds, scanned the room, trying to figure out where the hell he was. The ugly plastic chair, banged-up dresser from the seventies, and gold threadbare carpet clued him in quickly enough, and he let out a pent-up breath. He was in a crappy room in an unfamiliar town with no friends, no family, and no job. He flopped back on the mattress and rubbed his eyes. Guess it wasn't a nightmare.

He folded his arms behind his head. "Alrighty, then, what should we do now?" he inquired of the empty room. Of course, it didn't answer or even give a single goddamn hint. It mocked him with its silence. "Thanks a lot."

He continued to stare, not really seeing anything nor finding any answers to his dilemma. He wasn't going to get anything accomplished lying here. He sluggishly slid from the bed and made his way to the bathroom to take a shower. Maybe he'd head downtown and check out a few of the bars and restaurants. Grab something to eat, have a few cocktails, and see if any of them could use a bartender.

He hadn't done any bartending since he went to work for Lear Industries a couple of years back, but it had to be like riding a bike. He'd been quite a popular barkeep back in the day, if he did say so himself. He just needed to find a happening club, cash in on some good tips, and chill until he could figure out what he wanted to do next. If said bar served the gay community, or at the very least was gay-friendly, he could make a damn good living. He had charisma, knew how to work a crowd. Hey, and even if they weren't hiring, maybe he'd get lucky and find a hot, hard body that would make him forget all his woes, if only for the night. It sure as hell would be better than lying there staring up at a ceiling covered in God knows what all night long.

He took a quick shower, giving special attention to certain sensitive areas—it was always good to be prepared—then stood in front of the mirror with a towel secured around his hips.

He ran a critical eye over his reflection. He hadn't had a haircut in months, and his normally clean-shaven face had a week's worth of growth—totally sporting the rugged wild-man vibe. He turned his head from side to side and smiled. He liked the new look. Might not be the best for job hunting, but he had to admit it was perfect for man hunting.

"Screw it. I'll worry about a job tomorrow." He winked at his reflection. "Time to get laid."

After a little manscaping, some tight jeans, and an even tighter T-shirt, Murphy slipped into his loafers and headed out the door. The first blast of heat made him gasp and had him rethinking his plans. Eight o'clock at night and it was still hot as hell, and the humidity was out of control. Sweat-soaked and red skin wasn't the look he'd been going for. *Heatstroke is so not sexy*. He rushed back into his room for a quick change into a white tank top, bright green board shorts, and flip-flops, then tried again.

Murphy wandered along the sidewalk in the downtown district, the sounds of Jimmy Buffett, Kenny Chesney, and a reggae beat from the various clubs mixing and mingling in the crowded streets. As the sun began to dip below the horizon, the colorful storefronts, restaurants, and bars lit up the night in an array of flashing neon. Everywhere he looked, people were smiling and laughing, some swaying to the music and still others singing. The feel-good vibes floating in the air seeped into him, chasing away the last of his unease, and he found himself whistling and his steps lighter.

They got a whole lot lighter when he rounded the corner and spotted two college-frat-boy-looking guys stepping out of a club hand in hand. *Looks like my kind of place*. Murphy took a moment to check out the worn whitewashed sign that hung above the open door. A cartoonish pink flamingo on one foot holding a rainbow-colored umbrella stood to each side of the words Flaming Flamingos in a cursive script. It was garish and so ridiculous that Murphy couldn't help but chuckle. He shook his head and walked inside.

Surprise, surprise, the walls were painted neon pink, and the same gaudy flamingos from the sign were plastered on numerous posters. There was so much pink and glitter Murphy's jaw ached with how sickly sweet everything was. However, he did like the distressed white tables, exposed whitewashed beams, and ornately carved wood bar—also whitewashed. It was too bad they were lost in the sparklefest.

Techno thumped from hidden speakers, the beat pulsing in sync with the low lights above the dance floor at the back of the large open room. Several men shook, shimmied, and groped to the upbeat rhythm.

Murphy was as far from flamboyant as it got. He didn't own a single item of pink; no rhinestones, glitter, or ruffles could be found among his collection of T-shirts and jeans. Normally he went for places a little less flashy. His idea of a good time was hanging out at a sports bar, tossing back some craft beer, and enjoying a game or two of pool or darts. He didn't mind the occasional night out at a dance club. He had moves, especially when the lights dimmed and the music got nice and slow. He also liked his men as he liked his beer: robust, stout, and aged to perfection. A select few within Flaming Flamingos fit the bill, especially the tall, dark, and rugged-looking guy who towered over the other dancers.

Murphy stepped up to the bar, keeping the good-looking stranger in his peripheral vision.

"Hi, sweetie, I'm Rory. What can I get for you?" asked the blond twink tending bar. The way Rory raked his gaze up and down Murphy's body, he obviously wasn't talking about just booze.

The words printed across Rory's chest—*I'm Flaming*—said it all. Murphy wasn't the least bit interested in that type of flame. Still, he flashed the man a wide smile. He took a seat on one of the stools, turning it slightly to stare at Mr. Tall, Dark, and Rugged shaking the ass Murphy hoped to be tapping before the sun came up.

"I'll have a Guinness, Extra Stout, if you got it."

THE DANCE mix ended, morphing into a slow sensual tune. Joe swiped the back of his hand over his sweat-dampened brow and turned to head to the bar. Before he could make it two steps, someone grabbed his wrist and jerked him to a halt.

"Where are you going, handsome?"

Joe yanked his hand free. "Sorry, I don't slow dance."

"Aww, c'mon, baby, dance with me."

Joe cringed at the sound of the twink's high whiny voice and, even worse, the desperation in his eyes. "Sorry…." Shit, the dude had told him his name, but obviously it wasn't important enough to remember beyond the dance floor. "I gotta hit the john and grab a beer. There are plenty of other guys I'm sure would love to dance with you." He turned on his heel and slipped around the paired-up dancers before What's-his-name could start begging.

Normally he enjoyed coming to Flamingos. It was a fun place, the music hopping and the drinks reasonably priced. There used to be a good mix of men, but nowadays it seemed the young, flashy, and flamboyant outnumbered the rest of the patrons five to one. Not that he had a problem with effeminate men. He'd gotten one of the best blow jobs ever from a tiny dude in a floor-length gown and six-inch stilettos. It had been a bitch getting the waxy red lipstick off his nut sac, but it had been worth it. Still, he wanted something different tonight.

He slumped down on a stool at the end of the bar and waved to get Rory's attention, then yelled out, "Jack and Coke on the rocks."

Rory smiled a big dimpled grin and nodded.

Joe swiveled his stool and rested his elbows back on the bar, staring out at the dance floor. Being early, the place wasn't yet crowded, giving the men plenty of room to dance. Joe used the term loosely. It looked more like sex with clothes on. It wasn't his thing. He wasn't into public displays of porn, and tonight he wasn't into twinks, topping, or blow jobs. Tonight he was craving a different kind of delight. He was looking to be manhandled. He wanted someone strong, confident, and able to pound him through the mattress.

"Jack and Coke on the rocks," Rory announced behind Joe.

Joe turned his stool back around, stopping halfway when he spotted exactly the kind of treat he was looking for. Seated at the opposite end of the bar was a ruggedly good-looking man Joe had never seen before. Not just good-looking, but oh-my-God hot! Without taking his eyes from the vision before him for fear he'd disappear, Joe reached out blindly and grabbed his drink. He wiped the drool from his chin before wetting his suddenly dry throat.

The stranger had a head full of messy chestnut hair and a red tone to the stubble on his masculine jaw. His skin too pale to be local. Even working long hours inside, he'd have at least a bit of color on his face and arms, but he was all creamy, dreamy, and yummy, totally lickable. Joe caught enough of the man's body to know he was built like a brick shithouse. His tank top was tight against a broad chest and his arms were thick with well-defined muscles.

"Fuck me," he begged. "Please."

Kenny, one of the regular slutty boys, was groping the stranger, who looked less than impressed. In fact, he looked like he needed a little rescuing from the persistent little shit. Joe could do knight in shining armor.

Drink in hand, Joe pushed to his feet and strolled toward the man, sending up a little prayer that some of those bulging biceps were formed while doing mattress push-ups.

"Can I get another beer?" the stranger shouted to Rory as Joe approached.

"Put it on my tab," Joe informed Rory. Joe downed his drink and set the glass on the bar. "And I'll take another."

The stranger looked up at Joe with stunning greenish eyes flecked with gold, a slight smile curling his full lip. "Thanks."

Damn if that husky voice didn't cause Joe's toes to curl and his dick to twitch, already in full anticipation mode. "My pleasure." Joe returned the smile. He held the man's gaze, weighing his chances of skipping the pleasantries and drinks and heading straight to his king-size bed.

"Hey, mind your own business," Kenny whined and tried to push in between Joe and the object of his lust. "I was here first."

"Why don't you go bother someone else," Joe suggested without taking his eyes from the stranger. Their gazes locked, and the world seemed to melt away, a strong connection made. Kenny was obviously aware of it, too, or maybe it was the fact that both Joe and the stranger were completely ignoring him. Whatever it was, he must have finally gotten the hint, because he spun around and scurried off without another word.

"Alone at last," Joe commented with a sultry tone.

"Thanks for the save. I'm Murphy, and you are?" He held out his hand.

Joe shook the offered hand. "Nice to meet you, Murphy. I'm Joe." He nodded toward the empty stool next to Murphy. "Mind if I join you?"

Murphy raked his eyes up and down Joe's body. The way he licked his lips when his gaze landed on Joe's crotch made it glaringly obvious he felt the connection, too, and he liked what he saw.

"Be my guest."

Joe pulled out the stool and straddled it, making a point to have the bulge in his shorts proudly on display. "You're not from around here. I'd have remembered you," he drawled.

"Michigan."

"A Yank, huh? I hear you Michiganders can be a bit on the frigid side."

"You heard wrong. The temperature may get below zero, but that just means you have to engage in physical activities that provide warmth." Murphy's voice was seductive and telling. "You ever been to the D?"

"Nope, but I'm hoping to get a little D tonight," Joe said. No point in beating around the bush. He was horny.

Rory set their drinks down. He smiled at Joe, then glared at Murphy before moving down to tend to another customer.

Joe picked up his drink and took a small sip. "It seems you have made an enemy of our little Rory."

Murphy shrugged. "I didn't mean to offend him, but I wasn't interested. He's not my type."

"And just what is your type?"

Murphy brought his beer to his lips. "You," he replied, sounding confident as hell, then took a big gulp of beer.

"I was hoping you'd say that." Joe palmed his dick.

"Anything in particular you're looking for?"

Joe squeezed his cock, pushing up into his hand slightly. "I'd have thought that was pretty obvious."

Murphy took another long pull from his draft, then ran the tip of his finger along the foam on his upper lip. Joe groaned when Murphy sucked that finger into his mouth and pulled it out deliberately.

"Yeah, it's obvious, all right. I was just figuring we should discuss particulars. No sense wasting each other's time."

"Good point. Let's hear them."

"I work hard and play even harder. I prefer to top, but I'm not opposed to bottoming once in a while. I don't do bareback, never have, never will. I also don't do the awkward morning-after shit, and I don't cuddle."

Joe kept his features neutral, acting like he was considering Murphy's offer, when really what he wanted to do was jump up and down and scream hallelujah.

Unable to hold his excitement back a second longer, he downed his drink and slammed the glass on the bar. "Well, Murphy from Michigan, tonight is your lucky night. Finish your drink."

Murphy arched a brow. "And what, pray tell, makes me so lucky?"

Joe moved closer until his lips were against Murphy's ear, getting a whiff of spicy cologne and clean sweat. "Because I'm going to let you ride my ass as hard and fast as you want, and I live a short two-minute walk from here." He licked the shell of Murphy's ear, grinning at the shudder it produced. "Now drink up."

Murphy went to his feet. "Forget the drink, let's go."

Joe was out of his seat and pulling Murphy through the growing crowd without another word, feeling the big shit-eating grin spread across his face. He had the sneaking suspicion it wasn't only Murphy's lucky night.

Chapter Two

MURPHY'S SKIN tingled from the contact of Joe's hand in his, the sensation racing along his arm and exploding in the center of his groin. "I thought you said you lived close?"

"Impatient, are you?" Joe chuckled.

"I wasted a full mug of some very good beer. What do you think?"

"Point taken." Joe led him around a corner and down a narrow alleyway. A couple of feet into the darkness, Joe stopped and pinned him against the brick wall. Joe pushed his hips forward, his erection hard against Murphy's equally hard dick. "I like how eager you are," Joe growled.

Murphy slid both hands around to squeeze Joe's ass. "Yeah?"

Joe nipped at his bottom lip. "Oh yeah."

"Then you're going to love how eager I am when I'm fucking you through the mattress. Hope you don't have to work tomorrow." Murphy squeezed Joe's ass harder. "Actually, I don't really care if you have to work. This is mine."

Joe opened his mouth, but whatever he was about to say was lost in a deep rumbling moan as Murphy thrust his hips, smashing their erections together.

"You sure you can handle all this?" Joe finally said. He was rolling his hips against Murphy, and there was no doubt as to what he was implying. Hell, in the bar earlier, Murphy hadn't missed how impressive the man's bulge was. He also hadn't missed how remarkable Joe was. He was tall, at least six three or four, a good three inches taller than Murphy, and while Joe wasn't as bulky with muscle as Murphy, he was well-defined and there was power in those lean muscles.

Murphy pushed his right hand between their bodies and cupped Joe's package. Christ on a stick, it was thick and long and oh so very hard. "I can handle anything you can dish out. Tonight I'll be using this like a gearshift while I'm riding your fine ass."

Joe laughed. "Wow, I don't know if that's the cheesiest thing I've ever heard, or the hottest."

Rather than answering, Murphy grabbed Joe's hair, tugged his head down, and kissed him hard. Joe responded with enthusiasm, opening his mouth wide and giving as good as he got. They both tried to dominate the kiss, a clash of teeth, tongue, and lips. Murphy widened his stance and pressed his cock against Joe's thigh, humping a little as he continued to massage Joe's prick. Joe rewarded Murphy's efforts with another one of those dick-twitching, rumbling moans.

The kiss went on and on, the movements of their bodies harder, needier, until Murphy's knees went weak. He was so turned on, and if they didn't stop, he would be slamming Joe against the harsh brick wall and, consequences be damned, taking his sweet ass right here and now.

Murphy released his hold on Joe and ended the kiss, breathing harshly. "Gotta stop, man, unless you want to get brick burns."

Joe took a step back and ran his hand over his mouth, then slid it down his chest, farther still to his groin, and adjusted his dick. "As tempting as that sounds, I'd prefer carpet burns. Let's go."

The walk to Joe's place was brief but painful with a raging hard-on. Murphy breathed a sigh of relief when they stopped outside a brightly painted yellow bungalow and Joe unlocked a baby blue door. The instant they were inside, Murphy shoved Joe against the wall and buried his face in Joe's neck, taking in his intoxicating scent while licking, nipping, and kissing the salty flesh.

Joe moaned, burying both hands in Murphy's hair. "That feels good."

"You taste almost as good as you feel." Murphy licked a path down Joe's neck and dragged his teeth across Joe's collarbone.

Murphy slid his hand beneath Joe's T-shirt, pushed it up over the hard planes of his stomach, then his shoulders, down his strong, lean arms and off, kissing and tasting every inch of exposed flesh as he went.

"You going to fuck me right here?" Joe asked with a smirk on his face.

Murphy thought about it for a heartbeat. He couldn't wait to be engulfed in Joe's sweet, tight butt, but sometimes the buildup could be almost as rewarding as the orgasm.

"No, you're going to suck my cock right here," Murphy countered. "But don't you dare make me come. I want to blow when I'm buried balls-deep in your ass."

Joe arched a single brow. "I'll try to restrain myself, but the question is, can you?"

"I don't know. That will depend on your cocksucking skills."

"If there was a contest, I'd be the champion."

Murphy rolled them until his back was against the wall and Joe was standing in front of him. He laid a hand on Joe's shoulder, shoving him down. "Prove it."

Joe sank to his knees, holding Murphy's gaze, and he slowly slid Murphy's shorts down to expose his cock and balls.

Joe wrapped his long fingers around Murphy's shaft, pumping it gently a couple of times before he leaned forward and rubbed his stubbled cheek on Murphy's balls and up his prick. "You smell good enough to eat."

Murphy fisted Joe's hair, tipping his head back until Joe looked up at him. "You can gum, lick, and suck all you want, but watch those teeth."

Ignoring the firm hold Murphy had on him, Joe bent his head. "These?" he asked before brushing his pearly whites over the sensitive head of Murphy's cock.

Murphy shuddered and released Joe's hair. "Yeah, those."

Joe licked a wet trail up Murphy's shaft. His teasing tongue caused Murphy to whimper, which would've been embarrassing if he hadn't been so lost in the feel of that damn tongue dragging over the sensitive underside of his prick. He clenched his hands into fists to keep from grabbing Joe's hair again and taking that sexy, warm, wet mouth, hard and fast. *Have some restraint, dude.* It had obviously been far too long since he'd gotten off; a few swipes of a tongue and he was ready to blow like a randy teenager.

And didn't it get all the more difficult when Joe gave him a hint of a wicked smile before he parted his lips and took Murphy's prick into his mouth one achingly slow inch at a time. Murphy stared, transfixed, as his entire cock disappeared into Joe's mouth. When he'd left his motel room, he'd hoped to get laid, but holy shit he hadn't imagined just how lucky he would be. Not only did Joe have a hot body and tight ass, but he could deep-throat too? Oh yes, Joe was slowly becoming a fantasy come to life. Now, if his ass was as good as his mouth, Joe would be pure perfection.

Joe pulled off with an audible pop and gazed up at Murphy. "How's that restraint coming along?"

Murphy swallowed hard before he could answer. "Just fine. Now how about you use that perty mouth of yours for something other than talking?"

Joe obliged by taking Murphy's cock to the hilt, burying his nose in the short hairs.

"Oh, damn." Murphy shook with the effort it took not to give in to the urge to face-fuck Joe and blow his load down his throat.

Joe, true to his word, was a champion cocksucker, taking Murphy deep, swallowing around his prick before pulling back leisurely to tease the head with his talented tongue. Within a few short minutes, Murphy was trembling and panting and—oh sweet Jesus!

"Stop!" He pressed his hand against Joe's forehead. The instant Joe released his dick, Murphy grabbed the base and squeezed tight. "Damn, that was close."

"Told you I was talented," Joe exclaimed with a satisfied grin.

Murphy squeezed his eyes shut and panted. It took several seconds to tamp down the urgency. When he opened his eyes again, Joe's grin had grown wider.

He liked Joe's confidence, but he wasn't about to let him get too cocky. "No argument here. Now get those pants off."

Joe didn't argue. He immediately got to his feet, kicked off his sandals, and wriggled out of his shorts. If Joe's dick had been impressive tented beneath cotton and filling Murphy's hand, then the visual was beyond awe-inspiring. It was ruddy, the blue veins bulging, giving it a purple hue. The head flared and shone in the low light, and a single drop of fluid seeped from the small slit. His balls looked heavy, hanging low and looking just mouthwateringly yummy.

"You see something you like?" Joe drawled. He put his hands on his hips, rocking them and making that mammoth prick dance and bob.

"I'm liking everything I see." Murphy licked his lips, gaze settling on Joe's cock and sac. "Some things more than others."

"It's all yours. Well, at least for tonight it is."

Now that Murphy didn't have his dick or his tongue shoved down Joe's throat, he got his first glimpse of where he was. It was a one-room studio apartment. Thank God there were no telltale signs of the club he'd met Joe in, not a single hint of pink anywhere. It was decorated in beach tones of tan, white, and blue and appeared to be clean, but it was the large king-size bed that got Murphy's attention.

"Get on the bed. Lie on your back and spread your legs."

Joe stood, looking down at Murphy with a slight grin. He had a good three inches in height on him, but Murphy wasn't intimidated. He was too horny to care, and he wouldn't be denied.

"Now!"

Joe's grin turned to full-on brilliant, as if he'd been waiting for that response. He turned and strolled to the bed, lean hips swaying, and climbed on it. On his hands and knees in the center of the mattress, Joe looked back over his shoulder and shook his ass wantonly before taking the position Murphy had instructed.

Murphy didn't know what was going through Joe's mind while taunting him like that, but if his goal was to get Murphy riled up so he'd fuck that smirk off his face, he was about to get exactly what he wanted. Murphy tore off his tank top, tossing it haphazardly behind him before he stalked over to the bed.

Joe pointed to the nightstand. "Top drawer."

Murphy pulled open the drawer and found a battered tube of lube and a large number of condoms—small, medium, large, and extra-large. Murphy snatched a large one and the lube before arching a brow at Joe. Joe simply shrugged, not looking the least bit embarrassed or apologetic. Murphy started to make a snappy comment but decided against it. He really didn't care at this second if Joe had slept with the entire state of Florida. Right now, Joe's ass was all his.

He crawled between Joe's splayed legs and dropped the condom on his chest. "Open that."

While Joe did as he was told, Murphy popped the top on the lube and slicked up his fingers. "Showed you mine, now you can show me yours." Without elaborating, Murphy leaned down, and as he pressed the tip of one slick finger against Joe's hole, he sucked a ball into his mouth, rolling it on his tongue. Joe arched and let out a strangled sound, the high-pitched tone uncharacteristic of the husky-voiced man. After the initial shock, Joe bore down on Murphy's finger, trying to take more, but Murphy denied him that pleasure. Instead, he tapped his finger against the tight hole, teasing it while he continued to lick and suck, alternating between Joe's balls and cock.

"You're a tease," Joe groaned.

"Not even close," Murphy assured him. With the flat of his tongue, he licked a wet trail up to the ridge below the wide cockhead. "Just repaying the favor."

"What is that—"

Joe's words cut off when Murphy clamped his lips around the head and sucked hard at the same time, dipping his tongue into the little slit. Joe's flavor was slightly bitter, a little musky, and just pure delicious.

Murphy continued to feast greedily on Joe's pole until Joe cried out, "Uncle!" He fisted Murphy's hair, tugging. "Stop! Oh, shit, stop before I come," he pleaded.

Murphy took pity on him, letting Joe's dick slide out of his mouth. It was totally self-serving. Murphy wanted that ass clamping down on his dick while Joe blew his load.

"Damn." Joe grabbed the ornate spindles on the headboard, his grip so tight his knuckles were white as he took in harsh, gasping breaths.

Murphy sat back on his calves and snatched the condom from where it had fallen to the mattress. "Roll over and hold on."

"Give a man a minute to catch his breath."

"You can catch it later. Now roll over." Murphy popped Joe on the thigh to get him moving.

"Pushy bastard," Joe grumbled, but he rolled over, reestablished his hold on the headboard, and raised his ass.

Murphy bent and brushed his beard across Joe's asscheek, and he squirmed. Murphy did it again to the other cheek, then couldn't resist. He sank his teeth into the taut muscle of Joe's right buttcheek, not hard enough to break the skin, but enough, to Murphy's great delight, to make Joe yelp. He kissed the abused flesh and then sat back to roll the condom on. He loved edge play, but he wasn't sadistic or stupid. He knew that once he started stretching Joe's ass, Joe would be close again, and from the way he visibly vibrated, Murphy doubted he would last long.

The sounds pouring from Joe increased, echoing around the small room as Murphy pushed his finger into Joe's ass. Murphy's moans mingled with the pleasure-filled melody of how tight Joe was. His dick twitched in anticipation.

Okay, so he didn't have as much control as he bragged about, because he was stretching that sweet hole and already going to his knees while sliding the tip of his cock along the soft sac. Sparks of lust erupted across Murphy's nerve endings, his whole body tingling. He needed to be inside Joe, right now.

Murphy pulled his finger free and lined his cock up. He then took a firm cheek in each hand, pulled them apart, and groaned as he watched the head of his dick disappear into Joe.

"Damn, you have a fine ass. Hot and tight and—" Murphy's breath caught, and he tipped his head back, letting out a low growl when Joe shoved back hard, taking Murphy balls-deep.

"Would you shut up and fuck me, Murphy? I'm done playing, dammit!"

Murphy felt the growl in Joe's tone right down to his toes, and he was done too. Joe had stripped him of the last of his control. He splayed his hands on Joe's back, rising into a semisquat. He used the power in his legs to drill into Joe over and over again.

Skin slapping against skin, muscles flexing, moans, groans, pleas. It all became a blur of lust as Murphy continued to plow into Joe. And Joe might have been the one taking it up the ass, but he was far from pliant or submissive, pushing back to take each thrust deep, power against power until the bed was quaking.

"I'm going to come.... Can't.... I...." Joe shoved back one last time and then just howled.

Murphy gritted his teeth and continued to pound into Joe until he'd wrung out every drop of Joe's orgasm. Only then did Murphy give in to the demands of his body and come in long, drawn-out pulses, Joe's ass clamping down on his dick, holding it, wrecking Murphy. He held his breath and arched his back, lost in his pleasure until his vision darkened around the edges from lack of oxygen. He slumped forward, lying across Joe's sweat-slick back, gasping for air.

He clung to Joe until his breathing and heartbeat slowed, completely boneless. He barely had the strength to move, but somehow he managed. He dropped the condom in the waste can beneath the bedside table and then flopped down on his stomach and buried his face in the mattress. He was only slightly aware of movement next to him, thought he might have heard Joe say something, but Murphy wasn't sure and was too spent to try to figure it out or ask. He shut his eyes and melted into the bed. He'd worry about it later, or not at all.

Chapter Three

KNOCKING FOLLOWED by "Housekeeping" roused Murphy from his sleep. He slid from the bed and shuffled to the door. He opened it a crack. "I don't need anything, and for the love of God, don't wake me up so goddamn early."

"I apologize for the disturbance, sir," responded a meek-sounding female.

Murphy shut the door and leaned against it, guilt swirling around in his gut due to his outburst. He quickly opened the door and yelled out, "Sorry to snap at you," before closing it once again. It wasn't the maid's fault for his grumpiness. He'd stumbled to his room sometime before dawn but had been so exhausted he'd forgotten to put out the Do Not Disturb sign or pull the curtain, and the bright Florida sunshine was pouring into the room, practically blinding him. He ran his hands over his face and rubbed at his burning eyes. After a night of the most mind-blowing sex of his life, Murphy was worn out but oh so happy—at least he had been until he woke up and remembered where he was and his current situation.

"Oh right, no job and low on funds. Good morning, reality," he muttered. He sluggishly headed toward the bathroom.

After setting the taps on the shower, Murphy stood beneath the warm flow of water and moaned as it pulsed down on the aching muscles of his neck and back. He ran the bar of soap over his chest and stomach. When he lathered up his dick, images of Joe flashed in his mind: the way Joe had looked on his knees, those sweet lips sucking him off, the way his tight ass had felt clamping down on Murphy's dick. Murphy groaned, his cock hardening against his palm. It had been mere hours since he'd gotten off, but apparently the dire circumstances he found himself in meant little in the wake of his raging libido.

"Thank you, Joe."

Murphy took care of his morning needs, washing and rubbing one out at the same time. He'd always been really good at multitasking. Now that some of the stress—or rather, the pressure—was relieved, feeling much better than when he'd woken. He pulled the curtains, dropped the towel he'd secured around his waist to the floor, then kicked back on the bed with a newspaper. He flipped to the want ads and found the section for employment. He bypassed most of the ads, knowing some would take weeks, maybe even months before he'd get a callback. Plus, he was sure that once things were worked out on BMC's end, he'd be working a steady, well-paying job soon enough. What he needed now was something quick and temporary. He scanned until he found the ones seeking waitstaff and bartenders.

Murphy laughed out loud when he came across an ad seeking a bartender at the Flaming Flamingos. He was definitely a little too macho to be sporting pink and sparkles. He drew an X over it.

His cell chirped, and he picked it up from the nightstand. He checked the display and accepted the call. "Hi, Mom."

"Hey, sweetie. How's it going?"

"Ran into a bit of a snag, but other than that, I'm good."

"What do you mean snag?" she asked, a hint of concern in her voice.

Twenty-six years old and Mom still fretted and fussed over him like he was nine. "Lighten up, Ma, I'm fine, although I find myself jobless at the moment."

"What are you talking about? I thought everything was set for you to start Monday?"

"Yeah, I thought so, too, but I guess there was an issue with permits or something." Murphy sighed. "I'm sure they will be up and running soon." *I hope.*

"I told you it sounded too good to be true. You need to get your butt in that car and get back home. Vlasic is hiring."

"Mom, seriously, I'm not going to come back and take another factory job, and I damn sure ain't taking one that makes me smell like pickles."

"I thought you liked pickles?" She chuckled.

"Ha-ha, I do, just not the stinky vinegar kind."

"So what are you going to do?"

"Right now I'm going to take my newspaper and head down to the local coffee shop and see if I can find a job. I'll call you later, okay?"

"All right, keep me posted. Oh, and if it doesn't work out, you're more than welcome to move back into your old room."

"I'll keep that in mind."

"Do you need any money?"

"No, I'm okay for now, but thanks for offering. Love you."

"Love you too."

He ended the call and shook his head. Poor Mama Lola wasn't settling into the whole empty-nest thing very well. Murphy had been nineteen, the oldest kid, and on his own when Dad suddenly passed away from a heart attack. It had been rough on all of them, especially Mom. Nevertheless, she focused on Murphy and his three siblings, and because of her, they'd ended up happy and well-adjusted kids. She'd done an awesome job being both Mom and Dad. However, since Jenny, the youngest and only girl, went off to college last fall, Mom was going nuts. He really should call her more often.

He set his phone aside, picked up the paper, and shook it out. "But first, a job."

NEWSPAPER TUCKED under his arm, Murphy strolled down the sidewalk. He'd stopped by a couple of places he'd circled in the ads already but so far hadn't had any luck. One was looking for someone to take over a manager spot, but it wouldn't be available until fall when the current manager started classes. The other two openings had been filled the day before. Just his luck. He wasn't even going to give a second thought as to why he hadn't been available the day before, not unless he wanted to go to the next potential job with a raging hard-on. Scowling, he brushed away the hair from his sweat-dampened brow. Ten o'clock and he was already being steadily cooked alive. A stiff dick, clothes soaking wet, long hair, and scruffy beard. *Oh yeah, I'd hire me.*

He stopped outside a window with a large cup of steaming coffee in the center, and above it the word Kaffeinate printed in scrolling script that intertwined with the steam. "Perfect," he murmured and stepped inside.

The pleasing scent of freshly brewed coffee filled his nostrils, and even though he was sweating like a stuffed pig, his need to caffeinate—or rather Kaffeinate—was even more pressing. A blast of cool air hit Murphy's overheated skin and caused goose bumps to bloom on his arms and a shiver to run down his spine. It felt wonderful, and although the temperature inside the large café was just this side of chilly, the atmosphere was warm and welcoming. The bright cream walls sported numerous paintings of coffee cups in an array of bright and muted colors. Scarred hardwood floors, a high ceiling with exposed wood beams, and overstuffed leather couches along one wall gave the place a homey vibe. Small bistro tables and chairs as well as a wood-topped bar along the back completed the space. An upbeat tune played from a replica antique radio on a shelf among bottles of flavored syrups and white coffee mugs in a multitude of shapes and sizes.

One couple sat talking and sipping coffee at a table near the back, and a young man with platinum blond hair had his face buried in a book at another. The only other patron was a girl sitting on one of the couches, tapping away at the keys of her laptop. Not much business, though Murphy figured most people had already had their daily intake of coffee by this time.

A cherub-faced girl with bright blue braids greeted Murphy as he stepped up to the counter. "Good morning. Could I interest you in our drink of the day, chai tea latte?" she asked, flashing a sweet, friendly smile.

"Good morning." Murphy returned the grin. He studied the menu posted above the shelves. He had never been much into the overly priced fancy coffee drinks and hated the taste of tea, but he was a fan of very dark, very strong coffee. "No, thank you. I'll have a large black coffee and a glass of ice water, please."

"Right away, sir."

Murphy picked up a sealed cookie… thing and studied it. Organic and gluten-free. *Sounds positively disgusting*. He set it back down. Then he saw frosted cinnamon rolls the size of a saucer on a cake plate beneath a glass dome.

"Now we're talking," he mumbled.

"Excuse me?" the barista asked. She set a large mug of coffee and a glass of ice water down in front of Murphy.

He pointed to the rolls. "Are those organic and gluten-free too?"

She cocked her head and stared at him as if he was speaking in tongues.

"You know, like all healthy and shit," he clarified.

Her eyes brightened. "Oh, got you. No, those are from Mrs. Williams. This place used to be her bakery, and she uses the same recipe she has for more than thirty years. I don't think they were as health-crazy back then. I highly recommend them if you're not counting calories."

She raked her gaze up and down Murphy's body with an appreciative expression. "Not that you need to worry about that."

"Sold."

She pulled a tray from beneath the bar and set Murphy's drinks on it, then added a sweet roll. "I'm Kallie, by the way."

"Nice to meet you, Kallie. I'm Murphy."

"You're not from around these parts, are you."

"That obvious?"

"Yup." She pursed her lips and studied Murphy for a brief moment. "Ohio or Michigan, maybe Illinois."

"What makes you think that?"

"You've got that nasally sound to your accent."

Murphy nodded. "Michigander, born and bred."

Kallie wrinkled her pert little nose. "Eww, all that snow. I don't know how anyone could live through a winter without sun." She took in Murphy's body again and waggled her brows. "No worries, we'll get you out of those restrictive clothes and tanned up in no time. I'll be more than happy to give you tours of all the best places to sunbathe, if you'd like. I even know a couple very remote, very private nude beaches."

"Thanks, that's very kind. I'll keep that in mind," he responded, keeping his tone friendly, but not overly so. He didn't want to give her any hope of a date—or whatever it was she was fishing for. "What do I owe you?"

Kallie tapped on the cash register. "Five twenty-five."

Murphy pulled out the correct amount from his pocket and added a couple of bucks for a tip. "Thanks. It was very nice to meet you, Kallie."

"The pleasure was all mine, I'm sure."

Murphy nodded, then took the tray and settled at one of the tables near the window. While he drank his coffee and picked at the roll—he could see why Mrs. Williams had been in business so long; it was delicious—he studied the paper and made a few calls. Not a single damn prospect.

"Well, I do like pickles." He downed the last of his coffee.

"Would you like a refill?"

Murphy looked up at Kallie, who was holding a carafe of coffee. "Hit me up." He held up his mug.

"Anything else I can get you? Another sweet roll?"

"Nah, I'm good. Unless…." It was worth a shot. "You don't happen to know anyone around here who is hiring, do you? I'm a pretty good handyman, bartender, dishwasher. All-around jack-of-all-trades." He smiled. "I'm not picky."

"Are you serious?"

"Totally."

"Follow me," she squealed. Kallie rushed behind the bar, pulled out a stack of papers, and started rummaging through them.

"Are you telling me Kaffeinate is hiring?" A coffee shop in the bowels of hell wasn't his idea of a great career choice, but if he could start right away, maybe he'd collect a few bucks to keep him going until he found a better one. Hell, he loved coffee, especially free coffee. It could be a sweet second job.

Kallie didn't look up from the file. "No, but the boss is."

"Come again?" he asked in confusion.

"Mr. Sterling, that's the owner, he's been looking for someone to renovate the apartment upstairs." She snagged a crumpled sheet from the stack and handed it to Murphy.

Murphy studied the paper. It was a handwritten to-do list. Drywall, paint, new fixtures, and about another fifteen simple enough things listed. Number sixteen had him laughing. *Screw it. Use the place for storage.* "I take it the boss hasn't used it for storage yet?"

"Nope. He's been saying he was going to do the renovations on his own for, like, forever, which we all knew was ridiculous. He's renovating a beach house, and when he's not there, he's working here. The man doesn't have enough time to sleep as it is."

"Wow, he sounds like a workaholic."

Kallie sighed dramatically. "That's an understatement. He's a great guy, but not many people would know that since he's always fluttering from one thing to another. Never sits long enough to have a meaningful conversation with anyone."

Murphy handed her back the list. "Do you think he's serious about fixing it up? And if so, when could I start?"

"Joe—I mean, Mr. Sterling is off for a few days, and he did leave me in charge." Kallie tapped a painted nail on the counter, and a mischievous glint shone in her green eyes when she met Murphy's gaze. "Can you do the stuff on this list?" She held up the paper.

Murphy took the list again and studied it more closely this time. He was damn good with power tools. In high school his best friend's dad owned a construction company, and Murphy had spent many a summer as a gopher and all-around grunt. The money hadn't been great, but the skills he'd learned were invaluable. He could do anything from tiling to carpentry, electrical to plumbing.

He looked up at Kallie. "You ain't got anything more challenging?"

She clapped her hands. "Yay! You're hired."

Murphy felt like a load of bricks slid off his shoulders. He swallowed a relieved sigh and held out his hand. "Thank you very much." A thought occurred to him, and he narrowed his eyes. "You sure you can make this decision? The last thing on the list was to turn it into storage. Perhaps he has other plans. Maybe I should talk to Mr. Sterling first."

She took his outstretched hand and shook it. "Nope, he'll thank me. Trust me." She let go and hurried past him, rounding the bar to head toward a closed door. "Come back to the office and I'll get you a key. You can check out the apartment and make a list of what you'll need."

Murphy trailed after her, feeling a hell of a lot better than he had only moments before.

Computer girl glanced up as Murphy passed. He gave her a smile and a nod. The scowl he got in return didn't even make a dent in his good mood. He was young, he was good-looking, and he was once again gainfully employed, even if it was only temporarily. It meant he wouldn't have to go running back home.

Life was looking up in the Sunshine State.

Chapter Four

JOE FOLDED his hands behind his head and stared up at the ceiling. His damn internal clock was impossible to turn off, and it didn't have a Snooze button. Eight years he'd been getting up at 4:00 a.m., and now, even on his days off, he couldn't sleep in to save his life. This morning was no different, but it wasn't his ticktock that had him wide-awake and staring at nothing; it was the hard wood he was sporting. And not the I-gotta-piss kind, but the type that could only be produced by dreams of the naughty variety. *Damn Murphy and his sexy self anyway.*

It had been quite some time since anyone had affected Joe enough to make an appearance in his dreams. Fuck 'em and forget 'em had been his motto since…. Yeah, he wasn't even going to think about that irritating little shit.

Over the past two years, he'd stuck to his motto many, many, oh so many wonderful times, and he wasn't about to change his ways now. His success at work and getting the hell out of this tiny rented bungalow were the only things he had room for in his life at present. Damn good thing he loved being at the shop. In fact, being away from it for too long made him anxious. He had a great crew, trusted them implicitly, but he still felt out of sorts when he wasn't there. The only time he could concentrate on something else was while he was fucking or renovating his beach house.

Now, apparently, there was a new thing worthy of his focus: chestnut hair, red beard, and a strong, muscular body. Since Murphy had left his bed the morning before, he had thought of little else, and it was driving him crazy. He'd never given a thought to a random hookup once they'd left his bed. Well, he wasn't going to stand for it. He'd be damned if he was going to lie here and pine after a one-night stand, even if said one-night stand had given him the most mind-blowing orgasm he'd ever experienced. Oh, and the way Murphy filled him, the power in each of his thrusts, the soft porn sounds he made when coming, the look of bliss on his face when sated….

Joe shuddered and his dick twitched.

Stop it! Disgusted with himself, Joe threw off the covers and stomped toward the bathroom, still experiencing the delicious ache in his backside. "Damn Murphy and his sexy self anyway," he complained, this time giving voice to his irritation.

By six o'clock, hard-on taken care of, he was showered, dressed, and climbing the walls. He had a good mind to head to Kaffeinate. He'd do it, too, if he thought he could sneak in without Kallie catching him. She was a pint-sized thing, the top of her head barely reaching his chest, but she was feisty as hell. She'd make good on her threat to quit if he showed up to work before Monday.

"Vacation! Bah. I don't need a vacation. I need to work and get Murphy out of my goddamn head is what I need." And apparently a good shrink, seeing as he was talking to himself way more lately than he was comfortable with. He needed to get the hell out of the confines of his small place before the walls closed in on him.

He snatched up his keys and wallet, shoved them into the side pocket of his cargo shorts, grabbed his helmet, and headed out the door. He might as well put all his nervous energy to good use, painting or mudding or *something*, anything. He fired up his scooter and maneuvered easily through the deserted Sunday morning streets. At the end of the road, instead of turning east toward the beach like he should, he headed west. He reasoned that Kallie didn't say anything about stopping by for a cup of coffee before getting to work.

He pulled around to the alley behind the café and parked his scooter. He retrieved his keys from his pocket and started to go in through the back door, but Kallie's threat popped into his head and he pocketed them again. He shook his head at himself as he made his way around to the front of the building. He was kind of afraid of the mini-dictator.

Who was he kidding? He was totally scared of her. The biggest reason he let her boss him around was that he couldn't afford to lose her. She was a huge part of Kaffeinate's success. Not only did the customers love her, but she was nearly as dedicated to the place as he was.

Joe stepped inside Kaffeinate with a big grin on his face. The traffic in town might have been light, but it sure as hell wasn't inside the coffee shop. *Cha-ching.*

"Good morning, everyone," he exclaimed.

A chorus of "Morning, Joe" went up around the room from the regulars.

"Oh no you don't," Jeremy chastised when Joe stepped behind the bar. Jeremy set the coffee down in front of Doc, one of Joe's oldest and most predictable morning customers, and then crossed his arms over his chest. "You so much as serve one person and I am telling Kallie."

Joe narrowed his eyes. "You wouldn't dare."

"The hell I wouldn't. I promised her I'd tell her if you showed up."

Joe plucked a mug off the shelf and gave Jeremy a pleading look. "Aww, c'mon, us guys have to stick together."

"I would if I thought it would help my cause."

Joe grabbed the carafe and filled his mug. "Still haven't given up on getting in her pants, huh?"

Jeremy's cheeks turned pink. "I'm wearing her down. Now get out of here before she shows up and hangs us both up by our balls."

Joe cocked his head and looked up at the clock. "Wait a minute. Why are you here?" Kallie always opened the shop, while Jeremy worked the afternoon shift.

"She asked me to cover for her. She'll be busy with the new guy."

Joe took his coffee around to the customer side of the bar and perched on a stool. Jeremy wasn't the only one nervous about being caught. "We have a new guy?"

"Yeah, Kallie hired him yesterday. Said she was coming in early to meet him and get his list. She didn't say what time, but seeing as she's got that up-at-the-ass-crack-of-dawn schedule like yours, there is no telling when she told him to meet her."

"His list?" Joe asked in confusion.

Jeremy served another customer before responding. "Yeah, he's renovating the apartment upstairs."

"Whoa, wait a minute. She hired someone to take on that project?" Irritation skittered along Joe's spine. It wasn't that he was mad—wait, yes he was. Dammit, *he* was going to renovate it, right after…. He rolled his eyes at himself. He'd been saying that for… well, a damn long time. Who was he kidding? He didn't have time. However, it still irritated him that she'd do this without checking with him first. "Did she say who?" Joe could only pray it wouldn't cost him an arm. Knowing Kallie the way he did, it probably would and both legs too.

"Nope." He took Joe's mug and poured his brew into a to-go cup, then handed it to him. "Here. Now will you get the hell out of here and let me work? Boss gets a little cranky if I make the customers wait too long."

"I do not," Joe protested, accepting the cup. "I'm as gentle as a kitten. Besides, I want to talk to this new guy, go over the list with him."

"Kallie already went over what you wanted done to the apartment with him. You can meet him on Monday and check him out before he actually starts." Jeremy knocked on the bar in front of Joe and then stepped back and called out, "Everyone tell Joe goodbye."

"Bye, Joe!"

Apparently, getting a little cootie cat was more important than making the boss happy. He'd been where Jeremy was. Knew what it was like to lose your good sense when bitten by the lust bug. Well, not exactly the same. He'd never gone sniffing after the female species and never would. Joe wrinkled his nose at the thought. Still, he knew what Jeremy was going through—poor sap.

Joe took his coffee and got to his feet. "All right, all right, I know when I'm not wanted and outnumbered."

"Smart man. See you Monday, boss."

Joe hesitated. "You do realize I sign your paycheck."

"Yes, but you and I both know Kallie runs this place. Now shoo. I'm doing this for your own good."

"Yeah, yeah." Joe waved over his shoulder as he headed for the door. How in the hell had he ended up with not one but two employees who bossed him around? Hopefully the new guy would be on his side. However, seeing as Kallie hired him, the chances weren't in Joe's favor.

THE SCENT of old cooking odors, stale smoke, and a hint of mildew assaulted Murphy's nose when he stepped into the small apartment above Kaffeinate. Being closed up for six months with no air-conditioning had left the place stinky, but it was actually in much better shape than Murphy had anticipated, considering the lengthy list Kallie had given him.

The open floor plan gave the place a roomy feel, which it needed, considering the total space was only about seven hundred square feet. The place was in sore need of new flooring and paint. Other than that, it looked to be a pretty simple job. Some new lighting, maybe an island/bar to separate the kitchen from the living space, a little elbow grease, maybe sanding and painting the cupboards, and it would actually be a really great apartment.

Ideas popped in his head rapid fire, and he figured he'd best write them down or he was sure to forget them later. He jotted down a few notes, took some measurements with the tape he'd borrowed from Kallie, and moved into the bedroom. It was nothing special, four walls and seriously lacking in closet space, but he discovered hardwood floors beneath the thread-worn carpet, and it had a nice view of the street below out the large window.

He sketched out the floor plan, added a few more measurements, then went to check the last room. The instant Murphy opened the door to the bathroom, he found the source of the mildew stink. The dark, damp room was a breeding ground for mold and yuck.

"Total gut job."

He flipped the light on and immediately reconsidered. The old cast-iron claw-foot tub looked to be in great shape. The tile floor was cracked, the drywall would need to be replaced—as would the ugly sink—but the cabinet could be restored. Surprisingly the commode looked new, which would make his job a lot easier and save him time having to run downstairs every time he had to pee.

"Murphy? You in here?" Kallie called out from the front room.

"Yeah, be right out," he yelled back. He took the last of his measurements, stuck his pen behind his ear, and stepped out of the bathroom.

Kallie waved and smiled broadly. "How's it look? Having any regrets taking the job?"

Murphy shook his head. "Not a one. It's actually in much better shape than I thought. Looking at Mr. Sterling's list, I was expecting worse."

"He's a bit of a perfectionist," Kallie explained.

"Uh-oh."

Kallie waved a hand. "No uh-oh. I'm sure you'll do fine." She started opening and closing kitchen cupboards and drawers. "Besides, you're right. This place doesn't look bad at all. Smells nasty, but it's seriously not in bad shape. A little bleach, a little elbow grease, and he could have totally been banking rent."

"My thoughts exactly." Then something occurred to Murphy and he quickly ran some mental math. If he didn't have to pay rent, he could stretch out the money he had for quite some time, maybe even six to eight weeks. That surely would be plenty of time for his job to start. "Hey, you think Mr. Sterling would mind doing a little trade?"

Kallie turned and leaned against the counter. "What do you mean?"

"I'm in need of a place to stay until my permanent job starts. You think he'd be interested in trading labor for board? I'd flop here until the renovations were done."

"Ohhh, boss man's going to love you. Good-looking, handy, and cheap."

Exactly how I like my men too. He didn't say it out loud. He was simply keeping his naughty thoughts to himself. He never hid his sexuality, and he was always honest, but Kallie hadn't actually asked. He gave himself a mental pat on the back. Usually his brain filter was faulty on a good day.

"So you think he'll go for it?"

"Yeah, I know he will. Hell, he may even give me a raise." She smirked. "But anywhooo, I'm running late. They took longer than I thought," she said, shaking her fancy painted nails at him to indicate who it was that had taken so long. "Bring me your supply list when you're done, and I'll see what I can have available for you by tomorrow." Kallie moved to the door. "Oh, and help yourself to any cleaning supplies you need from the café. They are on a shelf in the storage room." With that, she was gone.

Murphy hopped up and sat on the counter as he took in the room around him, then nodded. It was a nice place, coffee always brewing a short staircase walk below. Maybe if the rent wasn't too high, he'd talk to Mr. Sterling about signing a lease once the reno was done. If not, he was sure he'd be able to find something reasonably priced or someone looking for a roommate. Either way, for the moment, there would be no tail tucking or thoughts of going back to Michigan.

Chapter Five

"OH SWEET Monday," Joe exclaimed the instant his eyes flew open. His pushy friends couldn't keep him out of his place today. He was going to have to do something about taking back a little power. He wasn't sure how, but maybe the new guy would even the playing field and be on Joe's side. He doubted it, but he could still hope.

He was showered, dressed, and out the door within fifteen minutes. His excitement caused his pulse to speed and a big silly grin to stretch across his face as he made his way to the café. Most mornings he enjoyed the quiet walk along the empty streets; however, he was simply too eager to get his day started and chose to take the scooter again instead. It wasn't as if he had to burn any extra calories this morning, and due to his constant pacing and jerking off—thanks to Murphy—Joe could afford to be a bit lazy one day. He was excited, dammit!

He parked in the alleyway behind the shop, got off the bike, and set his helmet on the seat. Satchel slung over his shoulder, he stepped up to the service entrance and unlocked the back door. He stepped inside, the big grin on his face growing even larger, and bumped the door shut with his hip.

"Good morning, old Kaffeinate café," he exclaimed. He dropped his bag on the floor. "Did you miss me?" Of course, the empty room didn't answer, but that did little to dampen Joe's happy mood. He loved this place. Kallie accused him of being a workaholic, but being within the walls of Kaffeinate never felt like a job. He loved the people—those who worked for him and those who patronized the coffee shop—and the scent of fresh-brewed coffee. He loved everything about the place and enjoyed it too much for it to be considered work.

Out in the main room, he fired up a café mix of music and shook his ass, dancing to the pleasing beat while he started the coffee to brew and set up the place for the early-morning rush. This was typically Kallie's job; Joe should be back in the office dealing with orders, bills, and payroll, but he didn't want to. He was in a great mood, and the last thing he wanted was to be stuck in the small windowless office. Not just yet, anyway.

Pen and pad in hand, Joe stood before the various flavors, taking an inventory. The music filling him, he grooved to the happy vibes.

"Hey, Joe."

Joe spun around, nearly falling on his face, his pad hitting the floor with a thud when he scrambled to get ahold of the bar.

Once he was steady on his feet, he laid his hand over his rapidly beating heart. "Jesus, Kallie. Give a man a heart attack."

"Sorry, I thought you heard me come in." She shimmied and swayed around to the other side of the bar. "Nice moves, boss."

He hooked an arm around her waist, bent, and kissed her on the top of her head. "Stop sucking up. You and I both know I have like zero rhythm."

"I wasn't sucking up. You're getting better." Extricating herself from Joe's hold, Kallie picked up the pad and handed it to him. Then she poured them each a cup of coffee. "Besides, what would I need to suck up for? You owe me."

"Thanks." He blew into his mug before taking a tentative sip. "What, pray tell, do I owe you for this time?" He pointed a warning finger at her before she could speak. "And don't you dare say for my forced vacation. I am not thanking you, nor do I owe you for your blackmail. If I was a smart man, I'd fire you," he threatened against his mug.

She waved one tiny hand dismissively. "You are a smart man; that's why you won't fire me. Besides, I was talking about the deal I got you on the renos. He's handy, cheap, and hot."

Joe moved around to the other side of the bar to get out of Kallie's way—she had her own way of setting up—and sat at one of the stools. "Uh-oh, this doesn't sound good for Jeremy," he commented.

"Jeremy has nothing to worry about. I simply said he was hot, not that he's my type. Too big and scruffy for me, but…." She spun around, eyes wide. "Oh. My. God. He's totally your type. Maybe he's gay. I should have asked him."

Joe held up his hands as if to ward off her evil suggestion. "Stop right there. I can hear the wheels in your head squeaking from here, and the answer is no! We agreed you would never try to play matchmaker ever again."

"But—"

"Shut it. Plus, no way would I ever date anyone that worked for me. That's just totally…." He pursed his lips. "Just no. I'm not looking to settle down, and if and when I do, I will find my own. Got it?"

Kallie shrugged and turned around to finish setting up the bar area. "Suit yourself."

Her words might have sounded like she wasn't going to try, but the mischievous tone had Joe nervous. She'd be finding out the new guy's sexuality the first chance she got, and if he was gay, heaven help Joe.

"I can't believe you hired someone to renovate the apartment without asking me. You really should have checked with me first."

"Why? You've been talking about it for months," she tossed back. "I simply helped you get another thing off your to-do list. You know how you love your lists."

"Yes, but I said I was going to do it."

"Seriously, Joe? When would you find the time to do it? Plus, when you find out how much you're paying him, you're probably going to want to give me a raise," she informed him, hands on her hips, preening, with a big satisfied grin on her face.

"How much?"

"Free."

Joe gawked at her. He couldn't have heard that right. "No, seriously, how much?"

Kallie leaned over the bar, pinched Joe's left earlobe, and pulled his head toward her. "Free," she repeated against his ear. "At least the labor part."

"How is that possible?"

Kallie patted his cheek and went back to her morning prep work. "He was looking for a place to stay, so he's willing to do the work as long as you provide the supplies and he can live in the apartment while he's renovating."

Joe gawked at her again. "You hired a homeless man?"

"You got issues with homeless people?"

"Well… no… it's just…." Joe sputtered. He didn't know what he meant, but the notion of Kallie just picking some random dude off the street didn't seem… kosher.

"Oh, simmer down. A homeless man didn't follow me home, nor was I cruising for one in the park." Kallie rolled her eyes. "Would you just trust me on this? I promise he's got credentials. He'll do a great job, I'm sure."

Joe sighed dramatically. "Do I really have a choice?"

"Nope."

"What's his name?"

"Eugene. He'll be here at ten. Now go do your bossy stuff and let me finish getting things ready."

"Like I'm actually the boss," Joe muttered. "Tell me again why I put up with you telling me what to do all the time?"

"Because you love me." Kallie leaned over the bar and pecked Joe on the nose. "Plus, I'm usually right."

"Yes, you are," he conceded, then held up a single finger. "When it comes to Kaffeinate, not my love life. So promise me if this Eugene guy is gay, you won't try to push him on me."

Kallie gave him an impressive pout that would probably send most men to their knees, vowing to do whatever she wanted. Hell, she didn't even have to pout, just bat her long lashes and Jeremy fell to his. Joe, on the other hand, wasn't most men, and since he wasn't buying what she was selling, he had more restraint when it came to her cute, pouty ways.

"Promise me," he said again.

Kallie threw up her hands in defeat. "Fine. Now shoo, shoo. I have work to do and so do you. Ohhhh, I'm a poet and didn't even know it."

The bells over the door jingled, and Joe turned his head to see Doc walk in. Even though they didn't open till five, Joe always left the door unlocked, knowing his old friend would show up promptly at four forty-five.

"Morning, Joe."

"Hey, Doc," Kallie called out. "Will you tell Joe I'm a great poet?"

Doc sat on the stool next to Joe. "Don't know anything about that. I know you're awful sassy."

"Ha, Doc's got your number."

Kallie stuck her tongue out.

"On that note, I've got some work to do." Joe picked up his coffee and stood. He patted Doc's arm. "Enjoy your morning." To Kallie, Joe said, "Yell if you need any help," and then headed to his office.

Kallie waved at him as she poured Doc's coffee. Joe walked into the kitchen to find Mrs. Williams unloading her sweet rolls. "Good morning, beautiful," he greeted.

"Morning, Joseph, dear. How was your vacation?"

"Horrible. I missed everyone, especially you, my Gracie," Joe informed her. He slid his arm around her plump waist and spun her. "Dance with me."

Mrs. Williams placed her hand in his and allowed him to twirl her around, laughing. He'd known her since before he could remember. Grace Williams was a big part of the reason he wanted to own his own shop. One of his fondest childhood memories was coming to her bakery on Saturday morning with his mom and dad. The fact that he always got a warm gooey sweet roll was only part of his enjoyment: the scents, the camaraderie of the neighbors who visited regularly just like him and his family, as well as Mrs. Williams's good nature and infectious smile.

When Mr. Williams died, Grace had decided to sell the place to Joe and retire. However, she couldn't stop baking, and lucky for Joe, too, because her presence as well as her sweet creations were a big hit in Kaffeinate.

Still laughing, Grace slapped at Joe playfully. "Turn me loose, silly boy. I have work to do and so do you."

"Why are all the women in my life always telling me what to do? Better question is, why do I feel compelled to obey?"

"Because we are usually right and know what's good for you," Grace replied with a wide smile that caused the corners of her eyes to crinkle.

"You've been talking to Kallie again, have you?" he accused.

"Taught that girl everything she knows."

"I'm doomed," he joked, and he pecked her cheek before doing as he was told. He could still hear her chuckling even after he'd closed the door to his office.

There was plenty to keep him busy, including paperwork to catch up on, one of the things he liked least about owning his business. Still, the good outweighed the bad, so he wasn't about to complain. He really needed to learn to keep on top of it, so then he wouldn't have to spend hours hunched over his desk once or twice a month, but that wasn't going to happen. He'd been saying it for years and still always left it to the last minute.

His stomach growled, and Joe looked up at the clock, surprised when he realized it was after nine. "Time flies when you're having fun," he said sarcastically.

Joe pushed out of his chair and stretched his arms over his head, his back protesting the imposed confinement with a series of pops and creaks. He rarely skipped breakfast, thanks to the dominant women in his life. Kallie and Grace wouldn't allow it. The shop must have really been hopping this morning if they'd forgotten to bring him something.

He stepped out of his office and hit something that felt like a brick wall. "What the fu—" His words died on his tongue when he realized it wasn't a wall, but…. "Murphy! Oh my God! What the hell are you doing here? I mean, it's good to see you, but I didn't expect to see you again. Especially not here." Joe cocked his head and looked down at Murphy in confusion and delight. "Seriously, what are you doing here?"

Murphy stared up at him, blinking, looking as stunned as Joe felt, although Joe's shock quickly turned into arousal when images of Murphy's naked body popped into his head. Joe's knees got all rubbery and he clutched at the door for support, hoping Murphy wouldn't notice the sudden swelling at his crotch.

"Well?"

"Kallie told me to be here at ten to meet the boss. What's your excuse?"

"I'm the boss."

Murphy's confused expression turned into something rather more cautious. "What do you mean, you're the boss?"

"This is my place, as in, I own it and the apartment upstairs."

The color drained out of Murphy's face. "You're fucking with me."

Nope, but I'd love for you to fuck with me again. They stood staring at each other, Joe's body thrumming with lust. Sure, he'd hoped he might see Murphy again, might have even prayed a little for something he rarely did these days—a second hot hookup with the same guy. However, when he realized he didn't know Murphy's last name, didn't have a phone number or know where he lived, he knew it wasn't likely to happen. And here he was in the flesh. Looking even sexier than Joe remembered.

At that moment, Kallie stepped around the corner, and her face lit up when she looked at Murphy. "Oh, I see you've met our newest employee, Murphy!"

"Kallie?" Joe's voice came out as a squeak, and he swallowed hard to clear his throat. "You said you hired someone named Eugene."

Murphy held out his hand. "Eugene Murphy. But don't you dare call me Eugene, or worse, Gene."

Kallie glanced back and forth between Joe and Murphy. "Do you two know each other?"

"No," Murphy said curtly. He pulled his hand from Joe's and stepped back. "Now if you'll excuse me for a moment, I need to hit the john."

Frowning, Kallie turned and watched Murphy leave. "What the hell was that all about?"

Joe shrugged. "I was coming out of the office and slammed into him. Guess he didn't appreciate it."

She narrowed her eyes. "That's weird. He seems so cool. A totally laid-back kind of—" Her eyes went wide, and she started to laugh. "Couldn't help yourself, could you? I told you he was hot."

"What?"

"You hit on him, and I'd say from his reaction, we now know his preference."

Yeah, he prefers condoms, topping, and doesn't cuddle. He kept that little tidbit to himself. "No, Kallie, I didn't hit on him." It wasn't a total lie. He hadn't hit on Murphy just now, and he wasn't about to discuss what had happened when he had come on to Murphy a few nights ago. She wouldn't appreciate hearing the hot, messy, sweaty details that had Joe's ass still aching.

Kallie's expression said she didn't entirely believe him, but she didn't push it. "He's a good guy and he needs the work, so do try to control your urges, hmm?"

Joe tried for an innocent expression. "I will do my best to keep the beast under control."

His attempt at innocence obviously hadn't gone over well—she arched a single brow at him. She shook one delicate finger under his nose. "Remember what you said? And I quote, fucking employees bad. So you keep that 'beast' of yours in your pants."

Too late. Forcing back the memories of Murphy sending him into sweet oblivion, Joe curled his hands beneath his armpits and hunched over like an ape. "Fucking employees bad, Joe good." He took it a step further by hopping up and down and grunting a pitiful-sounding ape impersonation that came out more like a chipmunk.

She patted his shoulder. "Good boy. Now go find yourself another banana to sniff after."

Laughing, Joe sauntered back into his office, his glee dying suddenly when images of Murphy's naked body flashed in his mind again, in vivid, high-definition detail. He was so doomed. He leaned against the wall, shut his eyes, and thought of the way Murphy had looked down at him with lust while Joe knelt at his feet. Joe's cock swelled and he swallowed a moan. He'd hoped for a repeat performance with Murphy because, seriously, getting fucked by the rough and rugged man definitely needed an encore. But Christ! He hadn't hoped for the man to stay right above his head or work for him. *Careful what you wish for.*

This could turn out really good, or really, really bad.

Chapter Six

"THIS IS bad, really bad." Murphy leaned against the closed bathroom door and scrubbed his hands over his face.

In a city the size of Tampa, what were the chances he'd end up not only running into Joe again, but actually working for him? Apparently, the odds were pretty damn good, considering he was standing in a bathroom that belonged to his new boss—Joe!

All right, pull yourself together, man. So what if the two of us hooked up. It was sex. It had nothing to do with the job.

Murphy nodded. He could do this. It wasn't like he was in a relationship with his boss. He'd hooked up with the guy one time. Didn't mean it would happen again or had to interfere with the work. He pushed off the door, went to the sink, and turned on the taps, splashed cold water on his face, and ran his wet fingers through his hair, smoothing it back.

He nodded again, this time at his reflection. "You can do this. You have to do this."

Feeling a bit more confident, Murphy stepped out of the bathroom and made his way down the hall to Joe's office. He stood outside the closed door and took a deep breath. He had no idea why his heart was trying to jump out of his chest or why his knees were shaking so hard.

Because you're being a pansy bitch.

"Shut up," he told his annoying inner voice. Being a pansy bitch had nothing to do with being nervous and everything to do with being a horny bastard and knowing he could give himself all the pep talks he wanted, but it wouldn't help. They sounded good but didn't mean shit. If Joe came on to him, Murphy wouldn't be able to resist, that much he was sure of. *God, please don't let Joe ask.* Murphy had it bad for his tall, sexy boss. *My boss!* "Ugh."

He'd popped a boner the instant he realized who had bumped into him. If Joe touched him again or gave him that sly grin, he wouldn't be able to concentrate on the renovation plans. He'd be too busy trying to

40

SJD Peterson

figure out how he could get Joe out of his clothes, bend him over the desk, and take him right then.

Damn, the way his tight ass felt around my cock. Murphy swallowed his moan, then took a few more deep breaths to get the overwhelming desire under control. His new mantra played over and over in his head— *You can do this. You have to do this*—until he started to believe it. He took one more deep breath, blew it slowly out, and knocked.

"C'mon in, it's open."

Murphy turned the knob and shoved the door open. His jaw nearly hit the floor and his breath hitched at the glorious sight before him. Joe was leaned back in his chair, feet propped up on his desk, looking cool, calm, and collected—all the things Murphy wasn't. And of course, Joe had that damn grin curling his full upper lip. But it wasn't the expression of ease or the smug smile that had Murphy reacting so strongly. Nope, it was the large tent in Joe's shorts that the bastard wasn't even trying to conceal.

"I, uh, I…." Murphy cleared his throat and tried again. "So, yeah, about the renovations."

Joe's smile widened. He set his feet on the floor and stood, then put his hands on his hips, long fingers framing his impressive bulge. "Is that what you really want to talk about at this exact moment?"

The hint of mischief in Joe's gray eyes caused Murphy's dick to twitch, and completely inappropriate thoughts swirled in his mind. He swallowed, trying to keep his focus, but with the suggestive tone in Joe's voice and the impressive dick on display, Murphy's brain was scrambled.

"Maybe another time would be better." He had to get out of there. Murphy turned to go, but his wrist was grabbed, stopping him before he could make it.

"No time like the present, I always say, and I have a very big, very hard job that needs the immediate attention of a good handyman." Joe pressed up against Murphy's back. "It's so good to see you." His warm breath tickled the flesh of Murphy's neck.

Murphy shivered. "I can't believe I'm saying this, but I need a job more than I need a fuck."

A deep rumble emitted from Joe, and he splayed his hand on Murphy's stomach. "Nothing says you can't have both. The job is yours if you want it. But I was thinking, before it was official, we could have a repeat of Friday night." Joe nuzzled Murphy's nape. "I'm not your boss yet, Murphy. Besides, you want me. I want you. I say we relieve a little of this tension sparking between us. Discuss the reno when we're more relaxed, less focused on our dicks."

Murphy tried to remember why this was a bad idea, but then Joe's hand slid down, the tips of his fingers brushing across the head of Murphy's overly sensitive dick, and he couldn't find a single reason not to take Joe up on his invitation.

Before thinking better of it, Murphy spun around, grabbed Joe's head in both hands, and captured those tempting lips in a bruising kiss. Joe moaned and fisted his hand in Murphy's hair. The smug bastard didn't even seem surprised. He ought to find that insulting, but he couldn't be bothered to worry about it now. He had other things to think about. Hard things. Warm, wet things.

Needing to exert a little dominance, Murphy ended the kiss and shoved Joe back. "What's everyone going to say when the boss steps out of his office walking with a hitch in his giddyup?"

Joe's eyes narrowed. To Murphy's surprise and absolute delight, Joe must not have cared what his staff thought about his ability or inability to walk because he stalked over to Murphy, pinned him against the wall, and took his mouth in another sizzling kiss. He let Joe think he was in control for a minute, content to let him dominate the moment while Murphy enjoyed the warmth of Joe's body against his, Joe's flavor on his tongue. Then all thought fled and Murphy forgot why he even cared who was in control when Joe fell to his knees and mouthed Murphy's crotch through his pants.

"Oh yeah," Murphy groaned.

Joe smiled up at him as his long talented fingers worked to unfasten Murphy's pants. "I was hoping I'd get another chance to taste you." Holding Murphy's gaze, Joe yanked the zipper open and shoved Murphy's pants and underwear down his thighs.

Rather than taking Murphy's prick into his mouth, Joe ran the tip of one finger gently up and down Murphy's shaft.

Murphy wanted more, needed more. He arched, thrusting into Joe's hand. "C'mon, stop teasing me and suck it."

One hand cupping Murphy's balls, Joe leaned forward and pressed his lips to Murphy's shaft. "Awful bossy, aren't you?"

"Yeah, you didn't have a problem with it the other night. Now shut up and get busy."

Joe chuckled darkly, but before Murphy could think about the tone or meaning behind it, Joe took the head of Murphy's cock into his mouth, sealing his lips around the head, sucking hard.

Murphy let out a strangled needy sound when Joe dipped his tongue into the small slit. "Oh yeah, just like that."

But apparently Joe had other plans. He winked and, rather than feasting on the head, took Murphy's entire cock deep into his throat, just swallowed him right down, and Murphy couldn't do anything other than thrust and moan and babble like a complete idiot for several ticks of the clock until his legs began to tremble, threatening to give out. Murphy threaded his fingers into Joe's hair, holding on, and locked down his legs. No way was he going to take the chance of falling and losing that warm, wet mouth. Murphy forgot about his plans to bend Joe over his desk, and all too soon he shot his release down Joe's throat. It took every bit of restraint he could muster not to roar out his pleasure. He bit down on his lip, the spark of pain enough to help hold back his shouts while he shuddered through each pulse of his orgasm.

The second Joe drew back and Murphy's cock slipped from his mouth, his knees did give out. He had to use the wall for support or he'd have ended up on his ass. "Damn, I needed that." He chuckled. "Give me a second and I'll keep my promise and bend you over your desk."

"Sorry, no time. Besides…." Rather than elaborating, Joe nodded toward his crotch.

Murphy glanced down. Joe's shorts were undone, his semihard cock exposed, one hand still wrapped around it, the other full of spunk. A snarky thought having to do with Joe's lack of control popped into Murphy's head, but instead of giving voice to it, he dropped to his knees, dragged Joe close, and kissed him soundly. Why? Murphy didn't have a clue and wasn't going to think about it at the moment, just like he wasn't going to acknowledge the butterflies that had taken flight in his belly or the way his heart had flip-flopped upon seeing Joe again.

Nope, he wasn't.

Nope.

Pushing to his feet, Murphy scanned the small cluttered office and spotted a box of Kleenex on a shelf. He pulled up his pants, tucked himself back in, and fastened up before grabbing the tissues.

He tossed them to Joe. "You cleaned me up. I guess it's only fair I repay the favor."

Joe caught the box easily. "Thanks, but I'm thinking I got the short end of the stick in the cleanup department."

Murphy started to say he'd make it up to him later but snapped his mouth shut. No way in hell was he going to set himself up to fall for anyone. *No complications.* "Hey, they're extra soft and absorbent. I could have gotten you one of those cheap-ass scratchy paper towels from the bathroom, so count your blessings."

Joe laughed while taking care of his mess, then rose to his feet and tucked his limp cock back into his shorts before zipping up. "You have a good point."

An awkward silence descended upon them, choking the bliss Murphy had felt only moments ago. "So, um, yeah. How about we discuss the renovations over a cup of coffee. You know, out in the café." Murphy didn't think he could stand to be closed in with Joe for a second longer. It was already beginning to feel too weird.

Joe studied him for another long moment and then nodded. He tossed the Kleenex in the trash can, then opened the door. "I'm going to piss. I'll meet you out there."

Unable to meet Joe's gaze, Murphy walked out of the office. Once in the hall, he stopped with his back to Joe. He didn't dare look at him. "Want me to order you something?" It scared him how little control he had around Joe.

"No, thank you. See you in a bit."

Joe's footsteps sounded behind him, and then the click of a door. Only then did Murphy square his shoulders and force himself to take one step at a time, refusing to acknowledge the shaking in his legs or the smile on his face that was totally Joe's fault. *Damn the sexy bastard all to hell.*

Chapter Seven

HOW MURPHY had made it through a full hour of sitting across from Joe and actually listening was beyond him. Perhaps it was his stubborn nature or the fact that Joe scared him a little. Either way, he'd done it. Plans set out, list in hand, Murphy got the hell out of the café and escaped back to his motel room as fast as he could.

He tried to convince himself it was because he had to check out of his room before they charged him for another day, but it was a lame excuse. He ran because he was a coward.

"Oh my God." He groaned, sitting down hard on the lumpy mattress. "Why in the hell did Joe have to be the one?"

What had he ever done to piss off the cosmos so badly that he now found himself working for a man who had picked him up in a random bar. That wasn't the worst part, because after finding out who Joe was, he still couldn't stop himself from shoving his dick down the man's throat again. In his office, no less.

Murphy rested his forearms on his knees and hung his head. He was so totally screwed, and not in a good way.

After his breakup with Dylan, he'd sworn he wouldn't even attempt to see anyone beyond a one-night stand until he had finished school, found a good job, and felt financially secure. Murphy refused to let someone make him feel guilty for working toward his dreams. He'd checked off school, potentially found the good job, but he was far from his third goal. He was flat broke. He should be running, should be out there right now looking for a place to stay and a different temporary job, but for some strange reason, he couldn't bring himself to move.

Something about Joe drew him like a moth to a flame. It was dangerous, it made no sense, and yet here he was, fluttering mindlessly. Perhaps it wasn't Joe at all, but Murphy's out-of-control libido. He'd already proven what little restraint he had when he hadn't been able to turn and walk out of Joe's office. He'd had no difficulty dropping his pants or blowing a load without a second thought.

What freaked Murphy out was the thought that maybe it was more than simple sexual attraction that kept him from running. It terrified him beyond all reason to feel this way about anyone. No good could come from it, for either of them.

But obviously he didn't care about the consequences, because he'd agreed to work for Joe.

Groaning, Murphy flopped onto his back, the heels of both hands pressed to his eyes. "You are such an idiot."

He'd allowed himself to be tempted into the thought of trying a sexual relationship beyond a random hookup with someone. It felt wrong and so right at the same time. What was really pissing him off was the fact that he was more than likely making a mountain out of a molehill. Because, seriously, maybe Joe wasn't the clinging whiny variety of man Murphy had been unfortunate enough to meet in the past.

Joe seemed reasonable, mentally stable—he hoped—and nice. In fact, Murphy hadn't stopped to think that it was quite possible Joe didn't want anything from him beyond a temporary fuckfest too. That maybe, just maybe, this time he wouldn't have to deal with the awkward breakup or the guilt after he moved on to another job, another place, another man.

That's it. He was totally making a bigger deal out of this than he needed to. Kallie had mentioned Joe was a workaholic. He probably wasn't looking for nor had time for a relationship. No "probably" about it. Joe, like the job, was a temporary thing, period. Murphy pushed to his feet and headed into the bathroom to gather up his shower kit.

But just to be on the safe side, no more sex, none, zero, zilch! Not with Joe. Sure, it was good, really good, but that didn't mean he couldn't find another hot and horny stranger to indulge in when he got the itch. It didn't have to be Joe, couldn't be as long as Joe was his boss, and that was that.

Satisfied with his new plan and his resolve, he brushed his teeth and splashed cool water on his face, then wandered back to pack up his meager belongings.

SLEEPING ON a hard and lumpy mattress sucked, but dozing in a sleeping bag on a hard floor increased the suckiness tenfold. But what the hell, it was free, so Murphy wasn't about to bitch… too much.

He stretched his arms over his head, groaning when the pain in his lower back shot up his spine. It took a lot more stretching and a hot shower for the ache to finally ease and he was ready to get started. It was demolition day. He loved tearing shit up, but first, coffee.

Dressed in nothing but a tank top and a pair of shorts—he was learning the Florida dress code quickly—Murphy tromped down the stairs. A blast of heat welcomed him when he stepped out onto the street. He still couldn't tolerate the heat too well but was getting used to it nevertheless. The hot, humid mornings? Nope. Maybe BWC had a night shift. Working during the nighttime hours seemed a whole lot smarter than during the blistering heat. Yes, he was whining, but Christ on a pogo stick, did it have to be so hot at 7:00 a.m.? The idea of a hot cup of coffee made him a little ill, but his need for caffeine outweighed all other discomfort.

Murphy hesitated with his hand on the door, unsure of whether he should enter Kaffeinate. He was confident in his resolve not to sleep with Joe again, but he wasn't sure if he was quite ready to test his willpower yet. He scanned the café: customers occupied many of the tables and bar stools, still more stood in line at the counter. Kallie was twittering productively from one customer to another in what appeared to be a chaotic dance. It was quite amusing to watch, and adding to Murphy's happiness—or rather, relief—there was no sight of the owner. He opened the door and went inside.

Murphy stood in line behind two middle-aged men in business suits. He couldn't imagine having to wear one in the dead of summer here. It had to be downright torturous. *Poor saps.*

"Good morning, sunshine," Kallie said with a wide grin as Murphy stepped up to the counter. "You know you don't have to wait in line. You're more than welcome to get your own cup of coffee."

"But then I wouldn't have the pleasure of a beautiful woman waiting on me."

"Oh, aren't you just a charmer. You have everything you need to get started this morning?"

"Got everything I need right here." Murphy held up his hands and wiggled his fingers. "Well, these and a large cup of strong black coffee."

"That I can help you with."

Murphy pulled out a couple of bucks from his pocket and set it on the counter.

Kallie returned with a mug of coffee and set it down. She shoved the money back toward Murphy. "Free coffee is one of the benefits of working for Joe. Grab a seat and I'll get you a sweet roll."

"That's not necessary."

"I didn't ask. You can't work on an empty stomach."

Before Murphy could protest further, Kallie plopped a plate in front of him and moved on to refill other mugs. Others were waiting in line behind him, so Murphy did as he was told. He shoved his money back into his pocket and took his coffee and breakfast to the one empty stool at the bar.

He absently munched on his roll while he fired up his cell phone and scrolled through his emails. A couple from Mom—he'd reply later. One from Dylan—delete. A ton of spam—delete, delete, delete. Unfortunately, nothing from BMC, nor any missed calls from them. He finished his breakfast while playing a couple of games of Candy Crush.

"Another cup of coffee to go?"

"Thanks, Kallie. I'd love to, but in this heat, don't know if I could handle it." Murphy didn't look up from his game.

"You should try iced coffee."

Murphy jerked, his phone hit the counter with a thud, and he looked up into Joe's smiling face. And dammit, didn't that husky voice do all kinds of delicious things to Murphy's body that he really didn't want happening at the moment and, quite honestly, bugged the shit out of him.

His irritation was enough to push down the lust, and he caught up to the conversation quick enough. "Iced coffee? Sounds disgusting."

"Why? I thought you liked coffee?"

"I do. Hot coffee," Murphy clarified.

"Hold on." Joe went to the brewing station.

Murphy refused to let his gaze drop farther than the back of Joe's head. He simply refused to give in to his carnal desires. Not with Joe. Perhaps it was time for him to hit the clubs, find a tight ass, and fuck all thought of Joe Sterling right out of his fool head. There had to be plenty of other hot bodies. It was Florida, for Christ's sake. His mood turning sour, Murphy snatched up his phone, powered it off, and shoved it into his pocket, his movements angry and jerky.

"What the hell is he up to, anyway?"

"Proving a point." Kallie shrugged. "You'll get used to it."

Murphy doubted it. He had no plans to be around Joe enough to get used to him or learn any of his adorable or annoying habits. Maybe tomorrow he'd get up and have his coffee—hot coffee—before Joe came in. There really was no sense in tempting fate.

"Here you go." Joe winked and set a drink down in front of Murphy. "You can thank me later."

Murphy eyed the black iced thingy suspiciously, avoiding Joe's gaze. "Thank you for what? No way in hell am I trying that."

"Aww, c'mon, Murphy, take a chance. You seem to be the type of guy who likes to live on the edge."

Murphy looked up and arched a brow at Joe. Before he thought better of it, he replied, "You know damn well I don't sit on the edge, but plunge in deep."

Guess the filter isn't working this morning.

Blessedly, Kallie had gone to take care of another customer and Murphy's voice had come out low enough that he wasn't overheard by the guy sitting next to him. At least, Murphy didn't detect any reaction from the stranger, which was more than he could say about Joe, whose deep rumbling laughter hit Murphy right in the—

Nope, he wasn't going to acknowledge that sensation. Instead, he picked up the blackened ice and took a long pull from the straw, gulping down a good amount.

"Well?"

Grudgingly, Murphy had to admit it was better than okay. It was delicious and refreshing and damn Joe and his smug face. "It's not bad," he said, purposely keeping his tone and expression neutral. He got to his feet. "I need to get to work. What do I owe you?"

"Not a thing. Got everything you need this morning?"

Murphy nodded.

"Need any help?"

"Nope. I'm good." He wasn't comfortable with free food and drinks, and Murphy slid a ten-dollar bill beneath his empty plate. "Tell Kallie I said thanks."

"Sure will."

Not willing to test his restraint around Joe for a second longer, Murphy grabbed his iced coffee and headed out the door without a glance back.

THE INTENSITY of the morning rush over, Joe leaned back against the counter and munched on a peanut butter granola bar Mrs. Williams had slipped into his pocket earlier.

"Thank you for the help, boss. Your popularity keeps growing, and we're going to have to think about expanding," Kallie praised.

"It's your popularity that's growing. Did you see the way that kid in the red tank was drooling while he stared at you? He better not let Jeremy catch him doing that."

Kallie rolled her eyes. "Me? Seriously? I actually considered running out and buying you a bib."

Joe cocked his head. "What the hell for?"

Kallie waved a dismissive hand. "Don't play coy with me, it *so* doesn't work. You're seriously going to try to deny you were drooling over the new handyman?"

"Whatever. You're imagining shit."

"Oh really? Honey, I was choking on the sexual tension that was swirling around you two."

Joe shoved off from the counter. "I'm not having this conversation."

Kallie held up her arms, shaking her fists toward the ceiling. "Yes!"

Joe tilted his head. "What the hell is wrong with you?"

"You proved her right," Doc pointed out.

Joe jerked his head in Doc's direction. "Private conversation here. Plus, she most certainly is not."

Doc and Kallie gave each other a high five, then just cackled. Joe crossed his arms over his chest and briefly considered stomping his foot but caught himself at the last second. He also knew better than to protest any further. He'd be damned if he would give the two of them any more fuel to use against him.

"You two enjoy yourselves. Some of us have work to do."

Their laughter followed him down the hall as he headed to his office. He closed the door behind himself and slumped down in his chair, a silly grin on his face. Of course Murphy set off all kinds of tingling sensations, but he hadn't been as bad as Kallie had let on. Besides, it wasn't totally his fault. The guy was hot as hell, and it didn't help that Joe knew Murphy was *scorching* hot in bed.

"Okay, maybe I did drool a little." He chuckled. But he could control himself, and from now on, he'd prove it. Murphy was officially off-limits.

Chapter Eight

FOR THE second day in a row, Murphy found himself standing outside Kaffeinate, peering through the door, looking for a familiar face. Relieved when he didn't spot Joe and equally pissed off by his cowardice, Murphy slung open the door and stepped inside. Being five thirty in the morning, the place was far less crowded than it had been the previous day.

"Look who's up all bright-eyed and bushy-tailed," Kallie said by way of greeting.

"I don't know about the bushy-tailed." He chuckled. "I figured I'd try to get as much done as I can before the sun comes up and cooks me." It wasn't a total lie. Even with the air-conditioning on high, the scorching Florida sun streaming through the curtainless windows heated the apartment to an uncomfortable temperature by noon. He took the empty seat next to Doc. "Morning, Doc."

"Morning. You know, you should try working at night and sleep during the day," Doc suggested.

"I'd actually thought about that, but I've come to realize it's way easier to work in an oven than to try and sleep in one. I'll be fine, just going to take a while to get used to this heat and humidity."

Kallie shook her head. "You'll never get used to it. Will he, Doc?"

"Nope," Doc replied without looking up from his newspaper.

"Great," Murphy grumbled.

"Cheer up." Kallie leaned over the counter and patted Murphy's arm. "The summer won't last forever—about as long as your Michigan winters."

"Not helping, Kallie."

"Sorry. How about I make it up to you with a cup of coffee and a sweet roll?"

Murphy scanned the area to make sure Joe hadn't shown up. When he didn't find him, Murphy leaned in closer. "Make it iced and all will be forgiven."

"Another one falls to Joe's persuasion."

Murphy narrowed his eyes. "The hell I did. It's too hot for regular coffee."

Kallie's face fell, and she held up her hands as if to ward off an attack. "Whoa, someone woke up on the wrong side of the bed."

"Oh shit! I'm sorry, Kallie. I didn't mean to snap at you. It's just... I'm a bit cranky before I've had my required amount of caffeine, and sleeping on a hard floor doesn't help either."

Kallie stared at him for a moment, as if she were trying to look beneath his skin to reveal his secrets. He held her gaze unerringly until she patted his hand and looked away. "One extra-large extra-strong iced coffee coming up."

Murphy let out a pent-up breath when she finally turned her back to him. It wasn't that his secrets were all that deep, and they certainly weren't dark—more like annoying. One secret he was working hard to eradicate along with the complications that came with it.

"She won't hold it against you. She's used to cranky men in the morning and knows how to make them happy."

"I take it that's why you're here?"

Doc picked up his mug and raised it toward Murphy. "Best service and coffee in town. It's the little things that make one most happy."

"I'll be sure to remember that."

"Be sure that you do," Doc said.

Murphy pointed to the newspaper on the bar. "Are you finished with that?"

"Help yourself."

Murphy flipped through the paper, pulled out the sports section, and held it up. "Yup, it's the little things."

Doc chuckled. "You're learning."

While waiting for his coffee and sweet roll, Murphy scanned through the sports articles. Typically he only followed hockey and football, but reading about golf and baseball was still better than getting depressed every day reading world news.

"I see you liked my recommendation."

Murphy jerked, nearly toppling his chair. "Dammit, Joe! Why in the hell do you keep sneaking up on me?"

Joe looked at him in confusion. "I merely set your drink down. You were expecting it, weren't you?"

"Yes, but from Kallie, not you," Murphy snapped. What the hell was it with Joe trying to give him a heart attack? *Annoying bastard.*

"Told you he was cranky." Kallie snickered as she passed behind Joe.

"Want to talk about it?" Joe offered. "I'm a great listener."

"No, I don't need to talk about it. I just need coffee, sheesh."

"He did bring you some," Doc pointed out. "Maybe you should just get it off your chest. No sense spending the day brooding."

Murphy snatched up his drink and sweet roll, then got to his feet. "You people are all crazy. I think I'll go enjoy my breakfast and caffeine in peace."

Doc patted Murphy's arm. "Simmer down, young'n. We were just messing with you."

"You're allowed." Murphy gestured to Joe with his head. "He's not."

"What the hell did I do?"

Gave me a boner. "You… well, you…. Never mind. You all have a good day. I have work to do."

"We're here for you, Murphy, if you ever need to talk," Kallie offered.

"Don't make me beat you," Murphy threatened. Joe started to open his mouth, and Murphy knew he was about to make a joke. Murphy would have, but he wasn't about to give Joe the chance. "You zip it, mister."

"Hey, I was only going to say it was my turn for these two knuckleheads to irritate me yesterday. Figured it was only fair today was your day. How about tomorrow we gang up on Kallie?"

Murphy looked at each of their smiling faces. "Like I said, you people are crazy." He turned and headed to the door, hiding the grin he could no longer hold back.

"See you tomorrow," Doc called out.

Murphy simply raised his cup without turning around.

Joe was making it increasingly difficult to keep him at arm's length. Problem was, Murphy wasn't sure if Joe was just a nice guy or if he was coming on to him. He wasn't going to think about the man, his sexy grin, and tempting body. He was heading out later and getting himself some ice trays, a coffeepot, and coffee grounds, and staying the hell away from any other kind of Joe.

UNFORTUNATELY, HE talked big but couldn't seem to get his mind or body behind the Joe-free plan. Three days of backbreaking labor, busting up tile and tearing down drywall, did very little to help him get Joe out of his head. But even if he could, it wouldn't matter. The bastard kept showing up in Murphy's dreams. And could the man do it just once in clothes? Nooooo. He'd woken with a full raging hard-on that morning and hadn't even been able to get up from his sleeping bag to pee until he relieved a little pressure.

Murphy had done his best to avoid Joe, going as far as to give him the cold shoulder the past two days. When he couldn't avoid him, he pretended he had other things on his mind. Truth was, little *but* Joe had been on his mind. He had to figure out how to deal with his new crazy obsession because he couldn't avoid Joe today—he was coming up to check on the progress of the renovations, choose flooring, and look at tile samples.

If Murphy listened to the whiny little voice in his head, he would talk to Joe about more than renovations. Part of him wanted to explain why—after Joe had sucked his dick… again—he'd shoved him away. Another part, the more rational and selfish part, argued to leave well enough alone, that no good could come of the conversation. The only thing the two battling sides could agree on was that he really should sit down with Joe and figure out a way to cut the tension built up around them. The thought made Murphy's stomach churn. He decided to stop thinking about it, at least until Joe showed up.

He checked his phone; Joe should be here any moment. Murphy stomped into the kitchen and washed his hands, then his face. And didn't it just irritate the living hell out of him when he caught himself fixing his hair and checking his clothes. Why did he care how he looked? Christ, he was a basket case. With an angry growl, he slapped the lever down on the faucet and dried his hands and face. The conversation he had to have was obviously making him more nervous than he should be. All the more reason to have it and get it out of the way. He was so done acting like a crazed lunatic.

After their little chitchat and the dust settled, not literally, mind you, maybe they could relieve any lingering tension with something a little more physical than talking.

Jebus, there you go talking with your dick again.

Murphy shrugged. His big head sure couldn't work the crap out— might as well let the little guy give it a go. He laughed and leaned his shoulder against the wall when he heard someone coming up the stairs.

He tried for a relaxed demeanor but wasn't sure if he could pull it off. Still, he tried. He rolled his neck to release some of the tension. When Joe walked through the door with that damn grin on his face, Murphy was sure he looked like a complete hot mess of nerves.

Any attempt Murphy made at looking casual flew out the window.

Joe was dressed in a pair of those ridiculous cargo shorts he always wore—black, this time—and a white tank top so tight that it showed off his pecs and each muscular ridge of his stomach.

"Wow! What a mess."

Yes, I am. Murphy pushed off the wall and stuck his hands in his pockets, feeling suddenly shy and unsure, which was stupid. "Yeah, well, we have to tear it down before we can rebuild."

"I suppose so. I'm just really surprised you have so much done. I'd have thought it would have taken a lot longer to strip this place." Joe brushed past him, taking in the room before wandering to the bedroom door and sticking his head in to check the progress in there as well. "Damn, Murphy, you're like a little workhorse, aren't you?"

Murphy couldn't help it. He actually preened a little after Joe's compliment. Then, disgusted with himself, he crossed his arms over his chest and glared at Joe's back. *How in the hell do you do that?* It was like the man walked in the door and Murphy turned into a virgin on her wedding night: a total bundle of nervous crazy.

"You don't know much about demo, do you." Murphy cringed when his tone came out testy. It was himself he was angry at, not Joe.

If Joe heard the harshness, he didn't point it out, the big goofy grin still on his face after he checked the bathroom. "You have no idea."

"What's that supposed to mean?"

"Never mind. I was just talking out loud. So you want to go over the swatches I brought?" Joe patted the messenger bag he had slung over his shoulder.

"Sure."

"Great!" Joe went to the floor in the center of the living space, sat cross-legged, and pulled out a stack of papers and brochures. "I was thinking we should go with a beach feel."

Murphy squatted in front of Joe, snatched a brochure on tile, choosing to look at it rather than meet Joe's gaze. "That's original," he snapped.

"Is something wrong? Have I done something to upset you?"

Great, he'd done it again, treated Joe like crap because Murphy couldn't control himself. It wasn't Joe's fault, and Murphy had no right to take it out on him. He still didn't understand why he should be so scared of having an honest conversation with Joe, but he was. He was terrified. Which, come to think of it, was pretty crazy.

After drawing a deep breath, Murphy let it out slowly, then finally met Joe's gaze. "No, you didn't do anything wrong. It's me. Got a lot on my mind today."

Joe laid his hand on Murphy's knee and held his gaze. "Anything you want to talk about?" Joe offered, sounding sincere.

"Nah, just silly stuff. Plus, I'm a little cranky. Woke up stiff this morning." *And not just my back.*

"The offer to sleep on my couch still stands. You don't have to sleep on the floor." The slow, sexy grin that always turned Murphy into a slack-jawed idiot spread over Joe's face.

We need to talk. We need to figure out how this is going to work between us. If we decide to be fuck buddies, we need to set boundaries and limits. Then, and only then, will I be getting in your bed, and it damn sure won't be for sleeping.

Murphy licked his lips. "Uh... I...."

Joe frowned. "Murphy? You okay?"

Murphy took a deep breath in a desperate bid to calm himself. Bad idea. Joe's spicy scent flooded his brain, and he was lost. He heard the growl rumble up from inside him, felt his palms plant themselves on Joe's warm shoulders, but he couldn't stop himself any more than he could stop the sun from rising in the morning.

Joe's bag and its contents scattered when Murphy shoved him onto his back. "Hey! What the hell has gotten into you, Murphy?"

Nothing is in *me, but I hope my dick will be inside you shortly. And it's all your fault, you sexy bastard.*

God, it made him angry to lose control like this. Stupid Joe, coming in here looking all flushed and gorgeous, making Murphy hard with nothing but his smug grin and his raw masculine scent and the growing fire in his eyes.

Without saying a word, Murphy ripped Joe's tank top off with a couple of swift, practiced movements. He then yanked the shorts down and off and tossed them behind him.

Joe let out a yelp as his clothes dragged over his privates, but Murphy ignored it. He wouldn't be distracted from his goal. He situated himself between Joe's legs, circled his thumb and forefinger around the base of Joe's half-erect cock, and took it deep into his mouth, sucking for all he was worth and moaning as he got the first taste of Joe's hot salty flavor.

"Oh wow," Joe gasped. His hips jerked, shoving his rapidly stiffening cock farther into Murphy's mouth, until his chin was resting on Joe's balls. Long fingers dug into Murphy's hair, pulling hard enough to hurt.

"That's it. Just like that. Feels good."

Murphy hummed around the head of Joe's cock, causing Joe's words to morph into low, husky moans. With his free hand, Murphy undid his jeans and fisted himself, then stroked. His rhythm was irregular, clumsy, but he didn't care. As long as Joe kept fucking his mouth and making those sweet, needy sounds, Murphy was in heaven. Jerking himself off probably wasn't even necessary. He could almost come just from the feel of Joe's prick stretching his mouth wide.

Joe's back arched, his shaft swelling incredibly larger in Murphy's throat. "Jesus, Murphy. You're going to make me come if you keep doing that."

Yeah, that's kind of the point, ya big lug. Murphy shut his eyes and redoubled his efforts, hollowing out his cheeks, working his tongue, and it only took another minute before Joe was shouting out his release and flooding Murphy's mouth and throat with his warm, rich spunk.

Several breaths later, Joe sighed, fingers raking through Murphy's hair. "Damn, Murphy, you'd give me a run for my money as cocksucking champion."

Surprised by the reverent tone of Joe's voice, Murphy opened his eyes and looked up. Joe's gaze locked with his, full of heat and tenderness. Joe's lips curved into that smile, the one that made Murphy's insides quiver, and it sent him tumbling over the edge. He came all over his thigh, his cries muffled by Joe's cock, which still filled his mouth.

His body was twitching with aftershocks when Joe tugged his prick free of Murphy's mouth, stood up, reached down, and hauled him up by the armpits. Murphy couldn't even find the energy to be indignant about such handling, which he figured said a lot about his state of mind right then.

Chuckling, Joe licked the remains of his come off Murphy's lips. "That was a compliment, baby."

Murphy scowled, feeling uncomfortable as hell after hearing Joe's choice of endearments. How, he wondered, was he supposed to stay detached, relegate Joe to the title of fuck buddy, if Joe was going to call him baby?

"Hey. Murphy." Joe ran his hands up and down Murphy's arms soothingly and stared down at him. Joe's smile remained in place, but unease shone in his eyes. "Okay, what's up with that scared deer in the headlights look?"

Murphy shook his head. "Nothing."

Joe continued to stare at Murphy. From the expression on his face, Murphy could tell he didn't believe him, but Joe didn't push. Instead he nodded and grabbed his shorts and shirt. "My offer to talk anytime still stands," he reminded Murphy. He wiped the mess from his leg with his shirt and slipped his shorts on.

Murphy stared at Joe's back, knowing he should say something, but he had no idea what. Half an hour ago, he'd known the answer to that question. Now, he wasn't so sure. As usual, Joe had thrown him completely offtrack without even trying.

"I want to know what is happening between us," Murphy blurted. "With…." He waved his hand back and forth between Joe and himself. "Us," he repeated, not even knowing where in the hell this was coming from or where it was going.

Joe blinked.

Murphy bit his lip before anything else stupid came out of his piehole. That hadn't been what he'd planned to ask. What he'd wanted to know was where Joe's head was. Murphy simply couldn't continue their physical relationship if Joe wanted more—like Murphy's heart. It wasn't up for grabs.

Just when Murphy was about to explain, Joe's shocked expression relaxed into that irritatingly sexy grin. "What do you *want* to happen between us?"

"If I knew, then I wouldn't be asking you, now would I?" Murphy snatched Joe's shirt from him and wiped up the mess on his leg before tossing it back to Joe. He fastened his pants, feeling ridiculous with his dick hanging out while Joe looked down at him.

"Simmer down."

Murphy glared at him for a few seconds and then huffed another harsh breath. "I'm cool."

"Uh-huh."

"Shut up," Murphy countered. "And why in the hell are you looking at me like that?"

Instead of answering Murphy's question, Joe said, "Come over to my place tonight." He raked a slow look down Murphy's body and back up again. "We can spend the entire evening in bed talking about us."

Murphy's eyes narrowed. "You and I both know if we get between the sheets there won't be a whole lot of talking beyond 'more,' 'yes,' 'harder.'"

Joe stepped up and pulled Murphy into an embrace. He then bent and kissed the end of Murphy's nose. "Fine, so we can fuck until we're both too tired to do anything but talk."

"Dude, if we go at it until I'm satisfied, I seriously doubt you'll be able to talk or walk." Murphy snorted.

"It's a chance I'm willing to take. So, you gonna come over after you're done here for the day? I'll even feed you."

"Yeah, I guess I can do that. I mean, I'm gonna get a meal and a fuck. What else could a man want?"

"You smartass." Joe took Murphy's butt in both hands and squeezed. "Good thing I like my ass smart."

"That's the worst compliment I've ever heard."

"Okay, okay." Joe chuckled. "So comedy isn't my strong point. You still going to share my bed tonight?"

"Well… that will depend on what you feed me."

"Cheeky bastard." Joe smacked Murphy's ass hard, then released him. He bent, stuffed the strewn papers into his bag, and shouldered it. "I'll see you tonight."

"Hey, I thought we were going to go over flooring and tile samples?" Murphy called out. He could hear Joe's footfalls on the stairs, but Joe didn't respond. Murphy put his hands on his hips and looked around the room. Once again, sex had become the priority rather than his good sense, and it was the floor that took a hit. "Well, damn, that's going to set reno behind." He tried to feel bad about it, but he couldn't.

Chapter Nine

JOE BLINKED in the dark, trying to place the unfamiliar sound that had woken him. He was spooned up against a warm naked body. Or was he dreaming? That was it, he had to be because it felt too good to be real. Then he heard the sound again and realization set in.

Murphy. Joe smiled. Murphy mumbled something Joe couldn't make out. His smile grew even wider when Murphy wriggled his ass closer against Joe's groin. He stifled a laugh by burying his face in Murphy's hair. His sweet Murphy, the same man who'd insisted more than once that he didn't snuggle, had his arms around one of Joe's, cuddling it across his chest. He briefly wondered if he should make Murphy aware of the fact that he was a cuddle whore when he slept but decided against it. Murphy would either not believe him, or worse, would then refuse to sleep in Joe's bed again. For now he would keep it as his little secret.

His eyes having adjusted to the low light trickling in from the hall, Joe pushed up on one elbow and peered down at Murphy's face. Eyes closed, features slack, making the cutest damn snuffling sounds Joe had ever heard. Murphy was a tough son of a bitch, and his attitude could be as gruff as his rugged looks. However, Joe was quickly learning there was so much more to him. He'd seen longing, lust, and confidence in those gorgeous hazel eyes. Yet he hadn't missed the look of uncertainty and shyness that at times would come over Murphy.

There was a lot about Murphy that Joe didn't know, hadn't really wanted to—at least that was what he'd been trying to convince himself. It scared him a little just how much he wanted to know in such a short amount of time of knowing him. But in Joe's experience, a little fear was a good thing. For now he'd keep it light and totally about sex like Murphy seemed to want. *Like* you *should want.*

"Like I do want," he reminded that little voice inside his head. There was nothing wrong with wanting to learn more of Murphy's secrets. Hell, maybe the knowledge would lead to even better sex, and more sex with Murphy?

Oh, yeah!

Speaking of which, he wondered how Murphy felt about wake-up sex.

But Joe's belly growled, and only then did he remember he hadn't kept the other half of his promise to Murphy. Not surprising, considering that minutes after Murphy had arrived at Joe's place, hands were roaming, clothes were disappearing, and it was *on*. No eating, no talking, just pure hot sex. Joe would be feeling it in an achingly wonderful way for days. But.... He pushed his groin closer to Murphy's ass, dick filling. Mmm, more sex, then he'd work on the promise. They had all night.

His plans set, he leaned down and brushed his lips against Murphy's ear. "Murphy," he whispered. "You awake?"

Murphy squeezed Joe's arm tighter. "No."

"C'mon, Murphy. I'm horny." Joe thrust his hips, letting Murphy feel how ready he was.

"You can't be serious," Murphy mumbled without opening his eyes. "Leave me alone. Sleeping here."

"You've been sleeping for like two hours." Joe rocked his hips and slid a hand down to cup Murphy's soft dick. "C'mon, baby, let's fuck again and then I'll bring you dinner in bed."

"You said that last time, and the only thing I got was a liquid protein diet."

"Hey, you told me to, and I quote, 'Do it, Joe, give me that sweet load.'"

Murphy cracked his eyes open. "I never said sweet."

"Yeah, well, you still begged for it." Joe laughed.

Murphy's brows stitched together. "I don't beg."

"Just like you don't cuddle?"

"Exactly." Murphy's frown deepened, and it must have dawned on him how they were lying, because he instantly released the hold he had on Joe's arm.

"So are you going to?"

"Do what?" Murphy snapped. He was obviously trying for grumpy, but the slight smile curling his upper lip ruined the effect.

"Fuck me?"

Murphy laid his hand over the one Joe had on his dick, rutting until he was every bit as hard as Joe.

He moaned when Joe curled his fingers around the shaft, stroking it in long firm pulls. "You're an insatiable bastard, aren't you?"

"Is that a bad thing?" Joe whispered against Murphy's ear.

Murphy turned his head and captured Joe's mouth in a brief kiss. "Nah, that's a very good thing."

"Yeah?"

"Oh yeah, because lucky for you, so am I."

"Good, because I plan on asking for it till your dick is raw and I can't walk."

"Pfft, won't be my dick falling off tonight. You're the one who woke me up, remember?"

"Yeah, what of it?"

Murphy rolled onto his belly. "You get to do all the hard work this time."

Joe gawked at the back of Murphy's head, trying to figure out any other way he could take Murphy's statement. He damn sure hadn't expected Murphy to want Joe to top him. Not that Joe had any issues with it—he loved to bottom, preferred it most of the time, but Murphy did have a hot little ass, and more importantly, Murphy wanted it and Joe would give him whatever he wanted.

"Well?" Murphy asked and wiggled his ass. This time Joe had no doubt as to what Murphy was asking for, especially when the man reached beneath his pillow, pulled out the battered tube of lube, and tossed it back toward Joe.

No way in hell was he going to question Murphy or miss a golden opportunity to have Murphy aching and walking a little funny—as Joe no doubt would be.

He snatched up the lube and poured a generous amount onto his fingers, slicking them up. "Roll over. I want to see your face."

"Stop telling me what to do." However, Murphy did as he was told, his hard cock straining toward his navel from between his parted legs. He wrapped his hand around it, stroking himself as he looked up at Joe with heavy-lidded eyes.

Joe's mouth watered as he looked over the feast laid out before him. He ran his clean hand along Murphy's thigh and cupped his heavy balls in the palm of his hand, then bent and nipped at the creamy skin on Murphy's prominent hip bone.

Murphy yelped and tried to squirm away. "That tickles."

Joe smiled and did it again, making a mental note of the sensitive spot. He planned to explore each and every last inch of Murphy's body, wanted to discover every hidden delight. Joe brushed his lips over Murphy's side. He responded with a hum and lifted his hips, his cock sliding along the side of Joe's bearded jaw. Joe smiled again when the gentle contact caused Murphy to shudder.

Joe pushed Murphy's knees up toward his chest, exposing that sweet little hole. He'd had a hot dream about rimming Murphy and aimed to make it a reality. He lowered his face and drew a deep breath. Murphy smelled like sweat and come, ripe and dirty, and God, beyond sexy. Fingers holding Murphy open, Joe dragged the flat of his tongue across Murphy's asshole. The salty-bitter taste went straight to Joe's groin, made his cock twitch. He groaned, Murphy echoed the sound, and Joe wondered if a guy could possibly come just from that sexy little noise.

He'd have to find out, but not tonight. He had other plans for Murphy. Joe darted his tongue out for one more taste before sitting back on his heels. "Damn, Murphy. You drive me to the edge faster than anyone ever has."

"Seriously, dude? It's not like you haven't gotten a nut today. Hell, it hasn't been that long since you got your second and already you're ready to blow just from licking my ass?" Joe shrugged, and Murphy sighed. "Horndog."

Murphy's tone was light and teasing, matching the sparkle in his eyes. Joe grinned at him. "Hey, this is totally your fault. Stop being so sexy and I might be able to control myself."

Murphy looked skeptical, but Joe held his gaze without so much as a slight smile. He was dead serious saying that Murphy was at fault. Mostly.

A few more heartbeats of standoff, then Murphy slid his arms under his knees and pulled them up to his chest. "All right, horndog. Get your cock in me before you come in your pants."

Joe started to make a witty comment about his lack of pants but snapped his mouth shut when Murphy glared at him. He was obviously done playing. Joe bit his lip and kept quiet, and slid a single slick finger into Murphy's hole.

"Yes," Murphy moaned, hands fisting in the covers. "More."

Happy to oblige, Joe pumped his finger in and out a couple of times before pulling it out and shoving two back in. He was rewarded with another low, rough moan.

Murphy shifted, pulling his knees back even farther, his hands curling into tight fists. He rocked, bearing down on Joe's fingers. Joe allowed Murphy to fuck himself on his fingers for a moment longer, until fluid glistened at the tip of Murphy's cock and the sounds coming from deep within Murphy's chest intensified.

"Don't come, baby. Want to be inside you first."

Murphy panted, hips rocking, then bit down on his bottom lip, eyes fluttering closed for a moment. "Okay, but you better hurry."

Joe pulled his fingers free, grabbed a condom from the bedside table, and rolled it on without taking his gaze from Murphy. A little more lube to his sheathed cock, and then he positioned the head at that sweet hole and pushed.

Once he was deep within Murphy, Murphy's ass clamping down on his cock, Joe gritted his teeth and went still as a tremor racked through him. He was dying to move, but he was half-afraid if he did, he'd be coming before they could even get a rhythm going.

With a frustrated sound, Murphy wrapped his legs around Joe, heels pressed against the small of Joe's back. The movement forced Joe's cock in deeper still. Pleasure jolted down Joe's spine, and he gasped.

"Move." Murphy rocked his hips. "Fuck me, goddammit!"

The growled command shattered the last of Joe's hesitation. He planted his hands on the bed near Murphy's armpits and pounded into him as hard as he could, spurred on by the pleasure-filled cries pouring from Murphy. He panted and moaned, muscles tensing with each snap of Joe's hips, his whole body begging for more. Joe gave it to him, each forceful stroke pulling another one of those sexy sounds from Murphy until the room echoed with them.

A knot formed at the base of Joe's spine. Orgasm coiling in his belly, he slid his hands beneath Murphy, holding on to his shoulders. They were pressed chest to chest, Murphy's cock trapped between their stomachs, their sweat-slick bodies sliding together.

"Come on, baby," Joe groaned, angling his thrusts to nail Murphy's gland. "Come for me."

Even though he'd half expected it, Joe was still surprised when Murphy came at his command. Murphy's ass clamped down on his cock as Murphy cried out something between indecipherable words and animal howl. Liquid heat poured from Murphy, covering their stomachs and chests, and it was one sensation too much for Joe. He came with his cock balls-deep in Murphy's ass and his face buried in the side of Murphy's neck, and it was so good he saw stars.

They lay together, both breathing harshly, hearts hammering. At least Joe's was, and he thought he could just lie here for like… forever. He was warm and tingling and bone-deep satisfied. Murphy allowed Joe a moment to enjoy his blissed-out state, but far too soon for Joe's liking, Murphy was pushing him off.

Joe grumbled and rolled, but the sound turned to a hum of delight when Murphy scooted over and draped himself over Joe's chest and leaned down for a slow lazy kiss. Winding his arms around Murphy's waist, Joe closed his eyes and sank into it. While lying on Murphy in a postorgasmic stupor, he hadn't thought it could get any better—he'd been wrong. Warm, naked, sticky bodies wrapped together, hands stroking as the kiss went on and on, was even better.

Murphy sighed against Joe's lips, then curled up in his arms, head resting in the crook of Joe's arm. "Okay, I think that…. Damn."

"That sums it up perfectly." Joe chuckled.

"I was going to say, would have been better had I not been so hungry."

When he caught the glint of laughter in Murphy's eyes, Joe's shock quickly changed to wanting to paddle the ass he'd just pounded. "You little shit." Joe reached for him, but Murphy anticipated it and was up and out of bed before Joe could grab him.

"Well, you did promise me dinner."

"Yeah. Dinner in bed." Joe grabbed for Murphy again, but Murphy laughed and jumped out of reach. "Wouldn't you rather have breakfast in bed?"

Shaking his head, Murphy held out his hand. "Nope. Now c'mon and get cleaned up so you can feed me."

"I can feed you something right now." Joe waggled his brows.

Murphy froze. "You've got to be kidding me. You actually think you could get it up again right now?"

Joe started to grab his dick, then noticed the condom. "I could, but you're right. Maybe we should clean up first."

Murphy tugged Joe's hand until he gave in and allowed Murphy to pull him from the bed. "I'll believe it when I see it."

"Don't tempt me or I'll prove it right now, mister."

"Tempt, tempt." Murphy snickered and headed toward the bathroom, hips just a-swaying.

Joe swatted that cocky little ass, and when Murphy spun around to glare at him, Joe snagged his wrists and pulled him close. "I really like your kind of temptation. In fact, I might even like you."

For a moment Murphy stared at him with an expression Joe couldn't read. He then craned his neck up and pecked Joe on the chin. "Stop trying to smooth-talk me. You're still feeding me, limpy."

They were still laughing when they stepped under the warm spray from the showerhead. Joe couldn't remember laughing so much or feeling so good with anyone like he did with Murphy. He had the uneasy sensation that he was falling for him. More than likely it was the mind-blowing sex he was falling hard for. He'd have to give that some thought later, but as hands roamed, lathering up arms and chests, the moment felt too perfect to say something to make it heavy, spewing feelings he wasn't sure he understood. There would be plenty of time to talk to Murphy about what was brewing between them.

At this moment, however, he was going to enjoy the cleanup, feed the man, and then *feed* him.

He had no doubt he could get it up again. Murphy's presence made it a surety.

Chapter Ten

REGARDLESS OF what Joe boasted, he hadn't been able to get it up again. It wasn't for lack of trying. The crazy son of a bitch spent more time teasing Murphy unmercifully than he did doing any actual washing. Murphy damn sure wasn't complaining. He didn't mind that Joe seemed unable to keep his hands off him.

After they got out of the shower, Joe headed to the kitchen to make good on his promise. "Wow, it smells amazing in here," Murphy commented upon entering the room.

From where he stood at the stove, Joe looked over his shoulder and gave him a dazzling smile that Murphy felt all the way down to his toes. "You're easy to please, aren't you?"

Murphy stepped close, pressing his chest against Joe's back, went up on tiptoe, and looked over his shoulder. "Not even close. Whatcha making?"

"Canned Italian wedding soup." Joe chortled.

Murphy pressed a kiss to the side of Joe's neck, then inhaled deeply. "Well, smells amazing. The soup does too."

Joe turned his head and begged a kiss, which Murphy gave him readily. He couldn't seem to deny Joe anything and was obviously suffering from the same problem Joe was. Murphy was having a really hard time keeping his hands off the man. It was so unlike him, it freaked him out a bit. Murphy knew he should be leaving before things got any further out of hand, but he simply couldn't seem to make himself walk away. Maybe after dinner he'd try again. He was starving.

"Soup will be ready in a minute. There's soda, water, or beer in the fridge if you're thirsty," Joe informed him, then went back to stirring the pot.

"Thanks. You want something?"

"Sure, I'll have a beer."

Murphy grabbed a couple of longnecks from the fridge, opened them, and set one on the counter next to Joe before taking a long pull from his.

"I did plan on making you a nice dinner, but you kind of distracted me," Joe chuckled.

"Me? Ha! That would be you, Mr. Grabby Hands."

Joe arched a brow. "I didn't see you complaining."

"Hard to do when a man has his tongue down my throat," Murphy countered teasingly.

"I do believe it was you who grabbed me and shoved *your tongue down my throat* seconds after you walked in."

Murphy waved a dismissive hand. "Technicality, Joe, technicality."

Joe laughed. "Uh-huh. Have a seat and I'll serve you."

"'Bout damn time," Murphy said with a big grin. He took a seat at the island and sipped his beer while Joe moved around the kitchen. It was all so domestic. A slight tingling of disquiet skittered down Murphy's spine. Joe's happy aura and smiling face helped dull the unease.

Joe set a bowl of steaming soup down in front of Murphy, then a plate of warm bread and butter. "I figured this would be a good time to go over swatches since eating might keep your hands busy," Joe informed him.

"Mine?" Murphy chuckled. "But, yeah, it's probably a good idea since you might be able to actually focus on something other than me."

"Doubt it, but what the hell, it's worth a shot." Joe winked, then headed out of the kitchen. A moment later he was back with his messenger bag. He took the seat next to Murphy and pulled out the swatches.

Unbelievably, they actually made it all the way through dinner without accosting each other. They settled on a manufactured hardwood, simple white subway tiles for the bathroom and kitchen backsplashes, and a black-and-white mosaic-type tile for the bathroom floor.

"I don't have any samples for kitchen cabinets, but I can get them for you in the next day or two," Joe said, then finished his beer. He held up the empty while getting to his feet. "I'm going to grab another. Want one?"

"Sure. There is nothing wrong with the kitchen cupboards. The Formica counters are hideous and definitely need to be replaced, but you'd save a ton by simply refinishing the cabinets. I'd paint them gray. It would be a nice contrast with the white tile."

"You know how to refinish those outdated things?"

Murphy washed down the last of his soup with the beer Joe had handed him and nodded. "Yeah, not much I can't do."

Joe's brows shot up.

"Construction-wise," Murphy clarified. "Plus, they're made of solid wood. It would cost a pretty penny to get anything of that quality made nowadays."

"Hey, look at you, saving me money. I might have to give you a raise."

Murphy snorted and grabbed his crotch for effect. "You raised me enough for one day."

"Not even close," Joe replied. He picked up the dirty dishes.

"I can get those. You cooked," Murphy offered.

"Nah, I got it. You enjoy your beer. You want dessert?"

"Depends on what you're offering."

Murphy's cell rang. He pulled his phone from his pocket and checked the display. He didn't recognize the number, but it had a Florida area code. *I better take this—it could be about my job.* "Hold that thought."

Murphy answered the call as he stepped out of the kitchen. "Hello."

"Hi, this is Donna Cohen from Barton Marlow Corporation. Could I speak with Eugene Murphy, please?"

"Speaking."

"I apologize for calling so late, but I wanted to let you know that the project you've been hired for is still on hold. Mr. Barton sends his apologies for the inconvenience and would like to offer you a job on another project until the difficulties with the resort are rectified."

Murphy frowned. *Difficulties?* He was curious about what she meant but didn't ask. At least they were offering him a job to tide him over. "That's awesome. When would he like me to begin?" A thought occurred to Murphy. "Wait, where is this job located?" He wasn't about to move again. First, he didn't have the funds, and second, he wasn't going to leave Joe hanging and back out on renovations now.

"Here in Tampa. We are upgrading the heating and cooling system at the Calm Winds Resort, and if you're interested, you could work with the crew for now. In fact, that's why I'm calling so late. They'd like you to report at 6:00 a.m., if possible."

Most big corporations wouldn't care about whether he was employed. The fact that they were offering him another job to see him through spoke volumes, and Murphy was thoroughly impressed with BMC's integrity.

He nodded. "That would be awesome. Do I need to bring anything?"

"No, sir. But I do need your consent to send your information to Fields, Fields, and Cohen. They own the resort you'll be working at. They will need to add you to their crew list and get you a badge."

"Absolutely. Thank you."

"You're welcome. Mr. Barton, the project manager, will meet you at the jobsite, and he'll go over all the details with you."

Murphy pumped his fist in the air. "I'll be there. Thank you so much."

"You're welcome. If you have any questions or concerns, please don't hesitate to call me."

When Murphy reentered the kitchen a few minutes later, Joe was finishing up the dishes. He looked over his shoulder at Murphy and smiled. Joe didn't ask who Murphy had been talking to, but the curiosity was clear as day on his face.

"That was Donna Cohen from Barton Marlow Corporation." Murphy took his seat at the island and picked up his beer. He held up the bottle. "Here's to going from no job to two."

"Barton Marlow Corporation?" Joe turned to lean against the counter and dried his hands as he stared strangely at Murphy. "The contracting company here in Tampa?"

"Yeah."

"Why are they calling you?" Joe frowned.

Murphy grinned. "About my job. It's why I'm in Tampa. I thought I was going to have to run back to Michigan with my tail between my legs. Now I won't have to. Yay, me!" Murphy tipped back his beer and took a big gulp. He felt better about his decision than he had in days. *This may just work out after all.* Poor Mama, she was going to have to get used to the empty nest.

Murphy was shocked when Joe crossed his arms over his chest, his face contorted into an angry sneer. "Murphy, you are not seriously considering taking a job with BMC?"

Murphy blinked, surprised by Joe's reaction. "Not only considering it, but have committed to it. I have to be at Calm Winds Resort at six in the morning."

Joe gaped. "What? You do know who they are working with, don't you? Who owns that resort?"

"Yeah, Fields, Fields, and Cohen." Murphy frowned when Joe's face turned an ugly shade of red. "What the hell's wrong with you, Joe?"

Joe laughed. It sounded strangled and a little hysterical. "Oh. My. God." Joe threw up his hands and stalked out of the room.

Murphy jumped up and followed him. "What's the matter with you?"

Joe didn't answer the question. He stomped to the front door and threw it open. "I think you should leave."

Murphy froze. "What?"

Joe glared at him. "You heard me. You need to leave."

"What's got you so pissed?"

Joe scowled, his chest rising and falling rapidly. When Murphy continued to stare at him, dumbfounded, Joe pointed. "I said, get the fuck out."

Murphy had no idea what was going on, and apparently Joe wasn't going to clue him in. Well, that was fine. If Joe wanted to be an asshole, Murphy could be one too.

"Fuck you very much for dinner," he spat and brushed past Joe. He jumped when the door slammed behind him. Murphy spun around and gaped at the closed door. Obviously, Joe's unexpected rage had something to do with the company that had hired Murphy. But the fact that Joe had aimed his dislike of a company at Murphy pissed him off to no end. Not caring if Joe was watching, Murphy shot a one-finger salute toward the front door before spinning on his heel.

Murphy would finish the job he'd agreed to do at that apartment. He wasn't going to be the same kind of asshole Joe was, even if the man deserved it. When he wasn't working, he'd spend his free minutes and find a permanent place to stay. Screw Joe. Or rather, someone else could, because Murphy wouldn't be touching or talking to the bastard again.

ARE YOU fucking kidding me? Fields, Fields, and Cohen.

Seeing red, Joe drew his arm back, ready to send his fist through the new drywall in the foyer. Instead, he squeezed his fist until his knuckles whitened and the muscles in his arm trembled with the restraint it took not to vent his rage on the wall. He needed several moments and even more deep breaths before the anger began to seep from him, and, in its place, despair to set in. Joe closed his eyes as a wave of nausea churned his gut. Could Murphy possibly not know how evil his new employer was? Deflated, Joe shuffled over to the couch and fell onto it. He rested his forearms on his knees and hung his head.

The notion that Murphy might not know how Fields, Fields, and Cohen had been suspected of ignoring laws, greasing palms, and poisoning the environment for years was ludicrous. Only someone in a bubble wouldn't know. FF&C had been in the national news for several years. The realization that Murphy could possibly know the evilness of the company and simply not care, that he would bow down to the almighty dollar, caused Joe's blood to boil again.

He pushed off the couch and, like a toddler in the midst of a righteous temper tantrum, stomped and fumed his way into the kitchen. He nearly pulled the handle off the fridge but gave no fucks. He was pissed.

Five years prior, FF&C had tried to take over the block where Kaffeinate was located. Joe had put every dime he had into his coffee shop, had busted his nuts working day and night to build a solid business and earn a good reputation with his customers. FF&C and their sneaky ways had nearly destroyed everything Joe had been trying to accomplish. He had only been saved because a few other business owners, those who had been there much longer than Joe, fought alongside him, and they were able to prevent the block from being demolished. In actuality it had come down to Mr. Edwards, whose shop had been one of the first general stores in the Tampa area, as well as Joe's building that had thwarted FF&C by having the properties registered as historical landmarks. It had been close, more like a last-minute stay of execution from the governor's office. Other areas of the city hadn't been so lucky.

Joe studied the contents of the fridge—beer wasn't going to help what ailed him. He slammed the door shut and headed for the liquor cabinet. A bottle of Jack probably wouldn't help either, but what the hell. It couldn't hurt.

The booze did neither.

An hour and three healthy drinks later, Joe sat on the couch staring at the distant wall, feeling a little numb and a whole lot disheartened. Not only because Murphy was working for a company Joe deemed as the enemy but also because of the way he'd treated Murphy. He should have given Murphy an opportunity to say something, to explain himself. Joe had simply reacted with rage, all logic and common sense fleeing his brain in its wake.

Sighing, Joe took another sip of Jack. He should call Murphy and apologize for his quick temper, but he didn't have his number programmed in his phone. *How can I not have his phone number?* He'd meant to save it; the paper with Murphy's number on it was sitting on Joe's desk. He smiled when he remembered what or, more aptly, who, had interrupted him, preventing the number from getting into his Contacts. The smile the memory produced quickly fell as guilt roiled in Joe's gut again.

He set his drink aside and got to his feet. He owed Murphy an apology. He shouldn't have treated him so harshly without giving the man a chance to explain why he was working for FF&C. Beyond the sex, Joe liked Murphy. He could see them becoming good friends. Murphy fit in with the type of people Joe liked to surround himself with. Kallie certainly seemed to have taken a shine to him. Problem was, if Murphy was, in fact, aware of the damage FF&C was doing and still planned to work for them, then Joe wasn't sure he could consider Murphy a friend. So he would talk to Murphy, hopefully make him realize the ramifications of working for a company that destroyed lives and would continue to do so, harming many more people.

But first, he needed to apologize for his own actions.

"C'MON, MURPHY, open the door." Joe banged on it again. "I know you're in there. Just give me a chance to apologize, please?"

Joe raised his arm when the door suddenly flew open and nearly knocked Murphy's forehead. "So apologize."

"I'm sorry, I—"

"Apology accepted. Goodbye."

Joe shot out his hand to stop Murphy from slamming the door in his face. "C'mon, Murphy, can we talk about what happened?"

"You were a complete and utter dick, you apologized, I agreed that you were a complete and utter dick, accepted your apology for being a complete and utter dick. Discussion over."

Murphy tried to shut the door again, but Joe refused to back down. Whatever the outcome of their friendship going forward, Joe didn't want Murphy to think such things about him. Even more importantly, Murphy needed to know everything about Fields, Fields, and Cohen and why Joe had reacted the way he had.

"I get it. I was acting like a dick."

Murphy's brow shot up.

"Complete and utter dick and I had no right to take my hatred for FF&C out on you."

"You were a total bastard," Murphy pointed out. He crossed his arms over his chest and glared at Joe, but at least he was no longer trying to take Joe out with the door.

"I know, and for that I can't say I'm sorry enough."

"Might as well come in." Murphy rolled his eyes and stepped back. "I mean, after all, this is your place."

Joe had thought he felt guilty before arriving. He had no idea what real guilt was until he spotted the sleeping bag and ruffled blankets on the floor in the corner of the living room. Turning from the sight, he faced Murphy. "There is no excuse for my behavior. No matter what I feel for FF&C, it gave me no right to treat you the way I did."

Murphy walked across the dusty room to lean against the counter in the kitchen. "What is your beef with them anyway?"

"How can you not know! They've been in the national news." Joe's ire began to rise, and he had to force it back down by taking several deep, calming breaths.

"I don't always follow the news."

Joe frowned.

Murphy obviously noticed and added, "Between working and going to school full-time, I had a hard enough time keeping up with what *I* was doing."

Joe's relief was great, as was his guilt. He'd judged Murphy before having all the facts. "FF&C has been trying to destroy this town and my business for years."

Murphy tilted his head, his brows stitched together. "Is this an issue of the mom-and-pop establishment against the devil that is corporate big business?"

"It's more than that, Murphy. They are coming here, forcing people to sell their life's work for pennies on the dollar. When anyone refuses, they sabotage their businesses, making it impossible for them to make a buck or to pay their staff." Joe leaned his shoulder against the wall and gazed into Murphy's thoughtful face. "That's not even the worst of it. It's a distinct possibility that Fields, Fields, and Cohen have no care for the environment. They have been accused of polluting the wetlands and burying it by using their wealth. They have some corrupt officials tucked in their back pockets."

Murphy's head shot up, his shocked gaze fixing on Joe's face. "You're not serious?"

"Quite so."

FF&C hadn't been convicted. They'd have to actually go to court first. But they had untold wealth to pay for the best attorneys who had used every trick in the book to institute one delay after another. Still, it was more than rumor and speculation. The Department of Natural Resources had proof, but until they could get the company into court, the arrogant bastards at FF&C were using the law when it suited them, claiming they were innocent until proven guilty.

"They haven't been convicted of any wrongdoing, but it's simply a matter of time."

"That doesn't sound very objective, Joe. How can you say that before you've heard both sides?"

Joe shrugged. "I don't need to be objective. I've experienced their shady bullshit firsthand."

Murphy looked dumbstruck for the second time, and Joe had a sinking feeling that he'd completely misjudged Murphy. "The people that I'm working for, who I drove all the way to Florida for…." He threw up his hands, his face turning red as he began to pace. "The same company I put my hopes in to fulfill my dreams is doing work with a company that tried to shut you down? Is that what you're telling me?"

Joe swallowed hard and nodded. He wasn't going to lie to Murphy. "Yes, but it was only due to the fact that we were able to get the buildings on my block listed in the historical registry. Had that not happened, they would have stolen Kaffeinate right out from under me. And I wasn't the only one who went to battle with them. A lot of other small companies weren't as fortunate as me."

Murphy let out a deep sigh. His face had gone pale when he finally stopped his pacing and stared at Joe with sorrow-filled eyes. "Jesus H. Christ, Joe. I had no idea. What the hell am I supposed to do?"

"You have a job at Kaffeinate if you want it," Joe offered, watching Murphy thoughtfully.

Murphy's eyes narrowed. A muscle in his jaw twitched. "I didn't go to school all that time to serve coffee for a living."

Ouch. Joe winced. "It was just an offer."

Murphy sighed again. "I didn't mean it that way."

"If it's because you don't want to be sleeping with your boss," Joe suggested cautiously.

"That's not it either, Joe. Don't you get it? This job is important to me. I may not have done my homework on Fields, Fields, and Cohen, but I did do it on the Barton Marlow Corporation, and they have an impeccable reputation. I can't believe they would be a party to underhanded practices like those that you're suggesting."

"I don't know about Barton Marlow, but I do know about—"

"Wait a minute. You're telling me all this anger and outrage is not because of my employer, but who my employer is being contracted by?"

"If you knowingly work for the devil, then you're no better than he."

There was no mistaking the expression on Murphy's face. He was pissed. Murphy stuck his chin out and held Joe's glare unerringly. "I am not going to argue with you about whether FF&C are evil as I don't have the facts, so I will have to take your word for it. But you don't have the same facts about Barton Marlow. You are judging them based solely on association, and that is unfair. So, listen up. I am going to continue to work for Barton Marlow because I'll be damned if I will go back on my commitment or give up the chance of a lifetime because you think that maybe, possibly, they are privy to the business decisions of FF&C." Murphy stomped across the floor and stood in front of Joe. He pointed a finger into Joe's chest. "They are a construction company, not a minion of the devil, and I'm working for them, got it?"

Joe stared, caught in a whirlwind of conflicting emotion. Murphy had a point, and as much as Joe hated to admit it, that point was valid. It still didn't diminish the unease Joe felt. Either directly or indirectly, Murphy would be involved with a company Joe loathed.

"But—"

"There is no but, Joe. If you hold this against me, it's like blaming the cow for moldy cheese."

Joe shook his head. "What?"

"Exactly. Now tell me I'm right and maybe I'll forgive you," Murphy demanded.

Joe had no clue what Murphy was talking about, and at the moment it didn't matter. Murphy was hot when he got all riled up, Joe's irritation was burned off by his growing arousal. He reached out, grabbed the back of Murphy's neck, and dragged him into a fierce kiss.

For a few heartbeats, Murphy didn't respond, his body tense against Joe's. Then, oh so slowly, he opened his mouth and allowed Joe's tongue in, his body arching and hands gripping Joe's shirt. Much to Joe's disappointment, it didn't last nearly long enough before Murphy turned his head away and broke out of Joe's embrace. He stepped back, breathing hard. Joe wanted to grab Murphy, pull him back into a tight hug, needed to feel him in his arms, but he didn't dare. He curled his hands into fists to keep from giving in to the need.

"Murphy—"

"Tell me I'm right," Murphy said again.

"You're right and I can't apologize enough for the way I reacted. Are we okay?"

"Yeah, I guess so. It's fine, I mean, it's not fine how you treated me, but I understand your reaction. I do. But, Joe, you can't hold this against me." He bit his lip, looking more uncertain than Joe had ever seen him. "We'll just have to agree to disagree."

"Okay, but will you make me one promise?" Joe asked.

"I can try."

"If you find out that Barton Marlow is knowingly and willingly breaking rules by order of FF&C, will you tell me?"

Murphy gritted his teeth, the muscles in his jaw once again twitching. "You want me to spy on my employer? Seriously, Joe?"

"Yes, I mean, not for the reasons you're thinking. I only meant…." Joe shook his head. "Never mind, you're right, I shouldn't ask this of you."

Murphy stepped up close to Joe. "Look, there is no proof of BMC's involvement in any wrongdoing, and if that changes, we will discuss it. That's all I can promise you at the moment."

"That's all I can ask." Joe closed the remaining distance between them and slid his arms around Murphy's waist. "How about a warm king-size bed instead of a sleeping bag."

"I don't know if I'm ready to forgive you yet, that whole utter dick move."

"Oh, I've moved up from a complete and utter dick."

"I wouldn't say that."

"So let me make it up to you."

Murphy still didn't look convinced.

"I'll even sleep on the couch if you want. You have to admit a real bed over the hard floor is a no-brainer. I'll even throw in breakfast."

Murphy pursed his lips. "You know damn good and well, if I come back over we'll end up in bed."

"And is that such a bad thing?"

Murphy stared at him for a moment. Joe didn't push. He'd apologized and was trying to make amends for his bad behavior. It was all he could do.

"Fine, you can make it up to me." Murphy untangled himself from Joe's arms and took a step back. "But no cuddling."

Joe was glad Murphy had turned around to pick up his bag. It made it much easier to hide the laughter that wanted to escape. No cuddling, huh? *We'll see about that.*

Murphy was a major cuddler, and thankfully he'd be the recipient of Murphy's noncuddling ways for the rest of the night.

Chapter Eleven

THE FIVE o'clock crowd—or rather lack thereof—was a welcome relief to Murphy when he stepped through the door of Kaffeinate. The past two days, he'd been working ten hours a day at the resort cleaning and assessing the ductwork, then spending his evenings tiling the apartment bathroom. He might have had a total of six hours of sleep, and the aroma of freshly brewed coffee started clearing the fog from his brain.

"Morning, Murphy. Have a seat." Joe nodded to the empty stool at the bar. "Hot or cold this morning?"

"Morning," Murphy responded sleepily. He plopped down heavily onto the stool. "I think I'll have it hot with my roll and an iced one to go, please."

"Coming right up."

Murphy scanned the area and found what he was looking for in a rack next to the register. He retrieved the newspaper and returned to his seat, pulled out the sports section and set the rest of the paper aside.

Joe set down Murphy's black coffee and cinnamon roll. "Anything exciting in the world of sports?"

"Won't be anything exciting till the fall," Murphy responded without looking up. He grabbed his mug and blew on the coffee before taking a tentative sip.

"Everything okay?"

"Just tired."

"You know, there is no deadline for the apartment. How about you take the night off and come hang out with me at the beach? I'll let you rub oil on my back."

"Tempting." Murphy chuckled. "But seriously. My first priority is to you. I promised I wouldn't leave you hanging."

"You're not. It would have been months, if not longer, before I would have gotten around to doing anything with that place. Although if you listen to Kallie, I never would have, so there is no rush to get it done."

Murphy took another sip of his coffee, then picked at his roll. "Okay, so, I'd feel better getting it done."

"Why? What's the big hurry?"

"Because I made a commitment and I'll get the job done," Murphy snapped. He instantly regretted it when Joe's face fell. "Sorry, just ignore me. I'm cranky before coffee."

Joe held up his hands and pursed his lips. "I'd say so. No more talking. I'll leave you to your brew." Joe turned away and headed to the other end of the bar.

"Joe...." But he'd already moved out of earshot and was serving another customer. Murphy sighed. It was true. He was cranky without his caffeine, and the lack of sleep only intensified his ill mood. But there was more to it.

He'd forgiven Joe for his outburst, but it had gotten Murphy thinking. The quarrel reminded him of why he wasn't looking for or willing to get hooked up in any kind of relationship. He didn't want anyone telling him what to do, making him feel guilty for trying to better himself. And it wasn't only the fight. Now that he was working in his chosen field, he had the opportunity to finally follow his dream and quite possibly make it come true.

He looked down to where Joe was talking with an elderly lady, a big smile on his face. *He'll only end up hating you.* The thought of it coming to that made Murphy physically ill. He was beginning to care about Joe, liked being around him, and if he were so inclined, could see himself falling for Joe. Maybe he had already begun the fall. However, he refused to continue down that path. He couldn't. He had to put the brakes on and take a step back. Better to keep things light between them. It was the only way to guarantee they would remain friends, something Murphy was sorely lacking in the Sunshine State.

"Refill?"

Murphy was pulled from his musings to find Kallie standing in front of him with a carafe. "Where did you come from?"

"Umm, I do believe I work here."

"I—"

"Just teasing. I was in the back getting supplies. How are you doing this morning?" Kallie asked as she moved to pour him more coffee.

Murphy waved her off. "No, thanks, I'm good, but can I get an iced one to go? I got to get to work."

"You look tired."

"I am, but nothing a little more coffee can't fix." He winked at her and popped a piece of his roll in his mouth.

"One iced very strong, very black coffee coming up," Kallie announced cheerfully.

While Kallie was gone to get his drink, Murphy finished his coffee and roll, all the while saying a little prayer Joe wouldn't come back. It was stupid and childish, and he seriously doubted the good Lord had time for such selfish prayers. But he said it anyway. He was a total head case and really didn't want to deal with his feelings for Joe at this time of morning. Plus, with as tired as he was and his trusty faulty filter, he'd only end up saying something he'd regret or, worse, hurting Joe.

"Here ya go, sweet cheeks. I hope it helps."

"Thanks, Kallie, and I'm sure it will." He pulled a couple of bills from his pocket and slid them under his empty plate.

Kallie frowned. "You know, that kind of defeats the purpose of free."

Murphy grabbed his drink and went to his feet. "Nothing in this world is free, darling."

"Wow, you really are not a morning person, are you? Skeptical much?"

"That's not what I meant. I tell you what, you stop being so literal and I'll try not to be skeptical. Deal?"

"Deal. Now get out of here and suck that thing down before you get to work. No one likes a crabby pants."

"I'm going." Murphy shot a glance in Joe's direction. Their eyes met and Murphy nodded. He then turned back to Kallie. "Tell him I said… um… yeah."

"I'll tell him." Kallie snickered.

Murphy glared at her. "Knock it off. I only meant tell him I'll see him and you tomorrow."

"Uh-huh. I'll tell him." Kallie puckered her lips, made an annoying smacking sound, and then blew. When Murphy only stood there and stared, Kallie's smile turned into a frown. "O-M-G, you didn't even try to catch it. Wait right there."

"Kallie! Where are you going?"

"Be right back," she called over her shoulder.

Murphy had a good mind to head out the door. He really wasn't into games this morning. He checked his watch. He'd give her two minutes. She was back in one, and Murphy couldn't help but laugh.

Kallie was holding a to-go tray with a cup full of ice and another cup three-quarters full of coffee. She took the drink from him, added it to the tray, and held it out to Murphy. "Here, Mr. Cranky Pants, finish the first one, and then add the ice to the other and drink it before you get to work. That should alleviate your CP."

Murphy started to respond, but Kallie interrupted him. "Doctor's orders."

"You're a nut ball," Murphy commented between snorts of laughter.

Kallie leaned in and pecked his cheek. "See you tomorrow."

As Murphy headed out the door, he was still in sore need of caffeine, but thanks to Kallie's bright smile and sweet disposition, he was beginning to feel less CP already. By the time he made it to the jobsite, he was smiling and whistling. He dropped his empty cups and tray into the trash and headed inside.

He frowned when he spotted Kent packing up his tools. "What's going on? We moving to another location?"

"I am. Mr. Barton wants to talk to you. He's out by the truck."

Murphy's gut twisted. Two days on the job and being called in by the boss couldn't be a good sign. With trepidation, he headed back out in search of Mr. Barton. Murphy found him in the parking lot, talking with a couple of crew members. Murphy waited patiently at a good distance, not wanting to interrupt or eavesdrop, although he would have loved to know what the boss was saying. From the expression on the crew's faces, it wasn't bad news, but that didn't mean Murphy would receive the same.

After a few tense moments, Mr. Barton spotted Murphy and waved him over.

"Good morning, son."

"Morning, sir. I understand you wanted to talk with me?"

"We're pretty much done here, so I'm pulling the crew to work on another project. The property owners have asked if I can spare a couple guys to assist their maintenance crew for a few weeks. I told them you and George would work well for them. George is experienced and you can learn a lot from him on repairing older systems."

Relief surged through Murphy. He still had a job. "Absolutely, sir."

"Great! I'll let Mr. Fields know. Report to the HR department, and they will get your paperwork complete."

An unsettled feeling came over Murphy, one even more pronounced than when he'd thought he'd be out of a job. "Paperwork, sir?"

"I'm subcontracting you and George out temporarily. If you want to get paid, I suggest you get that paperwork done." Mr. Barton's phone chirped. "I have to take this. Find George, he'll answer any questions you have."

"Thank you, sir."

Shit! After what Joe had told him about FF&C, the last thing Murphy wanted was to work for them directly, especially after he'd assured Joe he wasn't working for them, but for BMC. What the hell was he supposed to do now? His boss had chosen him for this job, and being the new guy with the crew, he didn't dare say no. Also, Mr. Barton did say it was only temporary. There was no reason to say anything to Joe. It would only upset him. Besides, it wasn't like they were a couple or anything. He didn't have to get the man's approval.

Murphy headed back inside to look for George. Even though he'd made the decision not to say anything to Joe, Murphy had a bad feeling about it. Or maybe it was his guilty conscience kicking up dust. He wasn't lying, he reminded himself. He simply wasn't going to say anything about who signed his paycheck. It was nobody's business but his own. He chewed on his decision for a moment, but it didn't taste very good. In fact, it tasted like shit.

MURPHY PUSHED his food around on his plate with his fork. He'd stopped at the first cabana bar he found after work, needing food and a beer. The beer was going down just fine. The food, on the other hand, not so much. The parting words from the lady in HR had been on his mind all day. *Welcome to the FF&C team.* Murphy couldn't help but feel like he was a traitor, which was silly, and yet….

"Is there something wrong with your seafood pasta?"

Murphy looked over and met the bartender's concerned eyes. "Nah, it's good. Just suddenly didn't feel very hungry. Can I get a to-go box and another beer?"

"Sure thing."

Murphy set his fork down and picked up his beer, downing the last of it while staring out at the ocean beyond. This was why he didn't want to get hooked up with anyone. He didn't want to consider anyone's feelings but his own. He had goals. He had dreams, dammit, and a healthy dose of guilt wasn't supposed to be part of his plan.

"One Bud, extra cold."

"Thanks." Murphy snatched up the bottle and guzzled half the beer.

"Whoa! Bad day, huh?"

"You have no idea."

"Well, tell ol' Gary all about your woes. I'm a great listener. Part of the job description."

"I'm letting someone get in the way of my dreams," Murphy complained.

"Uh-oh, this doesn't sound good."

"It's not."

"Hold that thought." Gary scraped Murphy's pasta into a Styrofoam container. "I'm going to put this in the fridge and get us a couple of drinks. Beer isn't going to help what ails you."

No, but maybe a lobotomy would. He was being ridiculous. Murphy barely knew Joe. Didn't owe him a damn thing. And yet he was considering the man's feelings in something he had nothing to do with. Insanity!

Gary rejoined him and set two shot glasses down in front of him. One with black fluid, the other white. "What's that?"

"A cure-all, better known as Jäger," Gary announced with a wink.

Murphy picked up the black one and sniffed it. "Eww, smells like black licorice."

"Tastes like it too."

"No, thanks. I don't like licorice."

"No one does." Gary chuckled. "That's what the coconut rum chaser is for. Trust me. A couple of these and you'll be so happy you'll be dancing on the bar."

Murphy wrinkled his nose and eyed the drinks suspiciously.

"Oh c'mon. Live a little. I tell you what. I'll have one with you." Gary poured two more shots. He held up the one with Jäger, then nodded toward Murphy's. "Bottoms up."

He might not like the taste of the drink, but if it was guaranteed to make him happy…. What the hell. Murphy picked up his shot and clinked it against Gary's. "Here's to dancing on the bar." He threw back his drink. The flavor was even worse than he'd thought it would be. He coughed and sputtered, his eyes watering.

Gary laughed boisterously and slapped Murphy on the back. "Do your chaser, silly man."

As soon as his coughing fit subsided, Murphy grabbed the rum and gulped it down. It helped, but the disgusting licorice flavor lingered on his tongue. "That has got to be the nastiest shit I've ever tasted."

"Oh, but the effects far outweigh the taste." Gary downed his rum, then slammed the glass on the bar. "Ready for another one?"

Murphy arched a brow. "Seriously? That stuff will put hair on your chest."

Gary raked his gaze down Murphy's torso and licked his lips seductively. "Yeah, I noticed. So, another?"

"Well, where I come from, it's only polite to repay the favor of a bought drink. Pour 'em."

"That's the spirit." Gary refilled the shot glasses. "Where are you from?"

"Detroit."

"Nobody's from Detroit."

"Only another Michigander would say that."

Gary smiled. "Born and raised in Farmington. Moved down here five years ago."

"No shit? I grew up in Southfield." Murphy raised his Jäger. "Here's to us being smart enough to get the hell out."

Gary clinked his glass against Murphy's and threw it back. The second drink was only marginally less disgusting than the first, but at least this time he didn't cough up a lung and had the good sense to quickly chase it with the rum. Gary had been right, though. The warmth in his belly and the pleasant buzz in his head was worth the taste.

Murphy didn't know about dancing on the bar. It was a good thing he didn't have to go back to work because a few more and he wasn't sure if he'd be walking very well, let alone shaking his groove thing. However, his foul mood was dissipating quickly. It felt good to be talking and laughing with someone he didn't want to bed or have an emotional attachment to. Although, from the way Gary was checking Murphy out, someone had fucking on their mind.

Chapter Twelve

MURPHY JERKED awake to the blaring of his alarm. Each shrill ring set off painful throbs in his head. He fumbled with the alarm, cursing when his sluggish fingers didn't respond quick enough. *Jäger.* Who in their right mind drank that stuff, and on a work night no less? Apparently, he hadn't been in his right mind because he'd done it, over and over and— he groaned—over again.

A thought occurred to him, and he quickly scanned the area. He sighed in relief when he found no one else in the room with him. He remembered talking and laughing with Gary well after the bartender's shift ended, recalled stumbling on the beach, trying to catch sea gulls. Oh, and his stupid attempt to swim in the surf, which would have been his undoing had Gary not pulled him out, but after that….

Nothing.

He didn't remember coming back to the apartment, but it must not have been all that long ago because his clothes were still damp. And while his head was pounding with the signs of an oncoming hangover, he could still feel the effects of the alcohol swimming around in his mind.

With great effort, he got himself to his feet. He was a little unsteady but made it to the bathroom without falling down or running into a wall. A hot shower and some coffee and he should be fine. The thought of coffee, of course, brought with it unwanted thoughts of Joe. He groaned and set the taps on the shower. What the hell was it about Joe that had him so messed up? He wasn't even sure he liked the man outside of bed… at least, that's what he kept trying to tell himself. He stepped beneath the warm flow and groaned again, this time with pleasure as the water pulsed down on his shoulders and back.

His evening at the cabana bar had been fun. He seriously needed to spend more time enjoying what the Florida nightlife had to offer and stop his insistent obsessing over Joe, especially now FF&C was directly signing his paychecks. Oh, and didn't that realization just make him feel all warm and fuzzy.

Not.

He snatched the soap from the tile shelf and scrubbed angrily at his chest and arms. This was all Joe's fault. Damn the man with his sly grin and hot ass, all the way to hell. He finished washing his body and then his hair, and with each tick of the clock, his mood became angrier and angrier. By the time he dried off, brushed his teeth, and got dressed, he was seething.

It didn't matter that it wasn't actually Joe's fault but Murphy's own inability to control his emotions and thoughts. He was still pissed at Joe nonetheless. Why did he have to be so charming, so good-looking, and so hot in bed? Why couldn't Murphy think about a goddamn cup of coffee without thinking about Joe?

"Goddamn you!" Murphy spat.

He found his wallet on the kitchen counter and snatched it up along with his cell phone. Today was a new day. Today he refused to let Joe dictate his mood or his actions. "I am my own man with my own needs and priorities."

Even as he said it, Murphy knew it was bullshit. Joe had worked some kind of mojo on him, and it was going to take more than some stupid statement to break the curse. He grabbed his keys and headed out the door. No, he wasn't going to Kaffeinate. He wasn't even going to walk by the door. Today he was going to Starbucks, and he wasn't going to get any damn iced coffee. Hardcore-strong black coffee hot was his goal.

"HAVE YOU seen Murphy this morning?"

Kallie looked up from her till and shook her head. "He didn't come in."

Joe looked upward. "Wonder if he's okay?"

"I heard him stomp down the back stairs earlier. Sounded like he was in a hurry."

"Hmm, he must have gotten up late," Joe surmised. "I'm going to do some paperwork. Yell if you need anything."

"Will do."

Joe went to his office and shut the door behind him before flopping down in his chair. It surprised him how disappointed he was that he hadn't gotten a chance to see Murphy this morning. Maybe he'd stop by the apartment later tonight and see how things were coming along.

Since Murphy had started working, Joe couldn't tell if he was telling him the truth about being exhausted or if he was trying to avoid Joe. He had the sneaking feeling that it was the latter. Murphy was a great guy, and he certainly didn't want there to be any enmity between them. They really needed to talk. A smile spread across his face when he remembered how it had gone the last time he'd planned on talking to Murphy. They had a hard time communicating but had no issues with physical stuff.

"If only the rest of life were that easy." He sighed.

Joe spent the rest of the day fluttering around the café, his head only partially on work. Annoyingly, he couldn't get Murphy out of his head long enough to concentrate on completing a task. He was simply going through the motions until Murphy returned to the apartment. Funny thing was, Joe wasn't sure he could explain why he was having such difficulties. He and Murphy fucked and fought—not really a good foundation for any kind of true relationship, whether that meant one in the true sense of the word, or just a friendship. What surprised Joe the most was that he'd contemplated pursuing the former, however briefly. What did he really know about Murphy? He knew nothing of his family, his likes and dislikes, hopes, dreams. The only thing he did know was the man could be funny as hell, made Joe laugh easily. Also, he was extremely attractive and an exceptional lover. Beyond that….

"I got nothing."

Joe tossed his pen on the desk and got to his feet. He hadn't written a damn thing in over an hour. He could no longer even pretend to work. It was time he got his shit together and figured out what was going on. They seemed to talk the most when there was something other than their dicks to concentrate on. *Food.* A couple of large pizzas should be a good buffer. Joe glanced at the clock: it was nearly six. Almost dinnertime. He grabbed his wallet and headed out.

One large pepperoni pizza and another with the works in hand, Joe stood outside the apartment door and took a deep breath before knocking.

Murphy opened the door, and his eyes went wide. "Joe, hey. I wasn't expecting… I mean—"

Joe held up the boxes. "I brought dinner."

Murphy hesitated for a second before stepping back. "C'mon in."

Joe stepped past Murphy and tried not to focus on his attire—or lack thereof. Murphy wore a pair of gray cotton shorts, his broad chest exposed. His skin was no longer as pale as it had been. The sun-kissed flesh begged to be explored with tongue and lips. Joe gave himself an internal shake. *Focus*. Joe forced his gaze from Murphy and took in the room. Tools lay scattered around the room, dust covered everything. However, where the place had been torn apart the last time Joe was here, he now saw evidence of rebuilding. Drywall had been hung and mudded, and an island was midbuild between the kitchen and living area.

Joe went to the kitchen and set the boxes on the stove. "Looks like you've been busy."

Murphy leaned against the wall. "It's coming along."

"I see that. You got any paper plates?" He opened a cupboard and found it empty.

"No, sorry, but there's some paper towels next to the fridge."

Joe glanced to where Murphy indicated, then back at Murphy. "You might want to put a shirt on."

"Why is that?"

"Because I was hoping to have a little pizza and conversation. If I have to stare at that mouthwatering chest and impressive stomach of yours, there will be little eating or talking being done."

Murphy crossed his arms over his chest. "So you think you can just show up here uninvited and start telling me what to do?"

"Yes, because I brought pizza. That automatically excuses any rudeness." He arched his brow. "Now, how about that shirt?"

Murphy pushed off the wall. "Fine. But I'm only giving in because you brought me food."

"You're so easy."

Murphy joined Joe in the kitchen a few seconds later wearing a bright yellow T-shirt displaying a large blue M. "I thought that was one of the things you liked about me."

"One of them." Joe wasn't going to think about the others at the moment because he'd been dead serious in his warning to Murphy. Joe was already hard and would forgo food for ass. Instead, he grabbed the paper towels, set the roll next to the boxes, then opened the box tops. "Wasn't sure what you liked on it, so I went extremes. Boring or supreme."

Murphy grabbed one of each, then hopped up and sat on the counter. "How'd you know I'd be home?" he asked before taking a big bite.

"I didn't, but I took a shot. I was hoping to get a chance to talk to you."

"About?"

Joe took a slice of supreme pizza, then leaned his hip against the counter. "It hit me today that we're either fucking or fighting, but I know very little about you."

Murphy froze with his pizza halfway to his mouth. "And?" His tone sounded suspicious.

"And nothing. I was just curious. Is that a bad thing?"

Murphy stared at Joe for a few seconds before he shrugged, still looking wary. "I guess not. What do you want to know?"

"Geez, Murphy, don't sound so enthused. I promise I'll take it easy on you."

"It's fine, ask me anything you want. Doesn't mean I'll answer it."

Murphy didn't sound like he was all that keen on Joe's reason for showing up at his place, but Murphy also hadn't said no or thrown Joe out, so Joe continued, keeping his promise.

"Any brothers or sisters?"

"Yeah, two brothers and one sister."

"Older? Younger?"

Murphy swallowed the bite he'd been chewing. "I'm the oldest."

"Are you close?"

"Yeah, I guess so. My dad died when I was nineteen. I'd already moved out, but I did my best to be there for them and my mom. She was pretty devastated, as you can imagine, but she really stepped up to the plate and took on the role as both Mom and Dad. When Jenny, the youngest and the only girl, went off to college last fall, Mom went a bit nuts. Not like in a 'lock her up in a padded room' extreme. She's simply not dealing with the whole empty-nest thing very well."

Joe could hear the genuine fondness in Murphy's tone as he spoke of his family. It said a lot about a man's character, one who cared deeply for his siblings and mother. The more Murphy talked about them, the more relaxed he became.

"My brother Rick is a drug rep, and Clinton is taking some time off from school to"—Murphy made the universal quote gesture with his fingers—"find himself. I don't believe it. His girlfriend took a job in Denver, and I'm pretty sure that's the real reason for his needing a break. I suspect he'll be transferring schools soon. What about you? Any siblings?"

"Nope, only child."

"I used to wish I was when I was still at home. Now I can't imagine how lonely that must have been."

It was Joe's turn to shrug. "I never thought about it back then. I was really close to my parents, and they always included me in whatever they were doing. We spent a lot of time on the beach or visiting the local establishments. They're the ones who instilled the love for this town in me."

"You said 'was' close to them. Did something happen?"

"They died."

"Oh. I'm sorry. I know what it's like to lose a parent, but both?" Murphy shook his head. "Man, I can't even imagine."

"It was rough." A swell of sadness rose in Joe's throat. He struggled to swallow it. He didn't want to get into a heavy emotional talk. He certainly didn't want to end up a blubbering mess by talking about how much he missed his parents. He wiped his mouth, then tossed his napkin in the trash. "You have anything cold to drink?"

"No, I was about to head down to the store and grab a few things when you showed up."

"I'll walk with you, if you want?"

"That would be great. Just let me grab my shoes." Murphy hopped off the counter, combined what was left of the two pizzas into one box, and stuck it in the fridge.

"That's not even right, man."

Murphy stopped midstep. "What's not right?"

"The way you abused that pizza. Don't you know you're supposed to hide it in the stove until morning?"

"And do what with it?"

"Eat it, obviously."

Murphy wrinkled his nose. "Umm, no. I'll refrigerate mine rather than take a chance with food poisoning, thank you very much."

"Pfft, the amount of preservatives in that stuff, you could probably leave it a week. It's not even real cheese," Joe assured him.

Murphy stared at Joe with a disapproving look, then turned without a word and disappeared into the bedroom.

Joe laughed. Well, that was one difference they'd have to agree to disagree on. The fact that Murphy was a compassionate man and could relate to losing a parent made up for any silly differences in food storage. It was an insignificant difference.

Murphy returned with his flip-flops on and his keys in his hand. "Ready?"

"Yup." He followed Murphy out the door and down the stairs. He was looking forward to learning more about Murphy and hopefully the likes would far outweigh the dislikes. So far, it was looking good.

They'd spent some time walking around, Joe pointed out his favorite places to eat and shop, as well as another bar he liked to frequent. They didn't go in. Joe enjoyed spending time with Murphy, talking about their childhoods and families, and didn't want to deal with loud music and crowds. Instead of a cold beer, Murphy had suggested a cold dessert. Of course, Joe knew the perfect place to get it. It was how they came to be here, sitting side by side, watching the sun go down.

Joe dropped his spoon into his cup and wiped his mouth with his napkin. "That was good." He bumped his shoulder against Murphy. "Great idea."

"I have them every now and then."

"I think you have them a lot. Look at the great ideas you came up with for the apartment. You also moved to Florida, which was the best."

"That remains to be seen."

"What more do you need to know? I mean, the weather is great: no more shoveling snow in the winter or driving on icy roads. Plus you met me, which makes that choice the greatest ever!" Joe boasted.

"Wow, ego much?"

Joe bumped Murphy again. "Hey, I am a great guy."

"Yeah, yeah." Murphy tried to hide his grin with another bite of ice cream.

Joe didn't point it out, just smiled back.

Chapter Thirteen

"WHERE WOULD you like these?"

Murphy spun around to find one of the deliverymen holding up two dining room chairs. His first thought was to reply to the stupid question with "In the bathroom," but figured it would just piss the guy off and Murphy would end up with scarred and damaged furniture.

"I'll take them, thanks."

He took the chairs and placed them with the small table they'd made room for in a nook next to the kitchen. There wasn't space for a proper-sized dining set. There would be no dinner parties served. But the seating would make a great area for whoever rented the place to have a cozy breakfast for two. A surge of sadness filled Murphy when he thought of someone else living in the apartment, but he had to face the very real possibility that it would be someone other than himself living within the freshly painted walls.

A new wall of windows had been installed to overlook the street below, giving the small space a much larger, airy feel. Dove-gray walls were the perfect contrast to the dark hardwood floors and black granite breakfast bar as well as the dark cappuccino-stained wood built-in shelves framing a big-screen TV. The sleek white leather furniture and throw pillows and prints in bright red, orange, and yellow gave the room a pop of color.

A few more pieces of furniture brought up and Murphy's work would be done. He stood in the center of the room, his chest swelling with pride at the transformation. Although he couldn't take all the credit. Kallie had turned out to be quite the impressive flipper. She had a few art pieces to hang, some knickknacks to arrange, and the place would be home-decorating-magazine-worthy. She had run out to pick up some fresh-cut flowers, stating the place needed a little feminine touch. Murphy disagreed—he liked the clean lines and masculine feel, but hell, who was he to argue with her? The place looked amazing.

Too bad the renovating going on inside Murphy hadn't gone as well.

He'd accepted the job from Fields, Fields, and Cohen, even after knowing what he did. His reasoning had been that it was a temporary position, one in which he could learn a lot, until the project got under way with BMC. He should have told Joe, but quite honestly, he was a coward. He also had to consider that perhaps it wasn't so much being afraid of what Joe would say or do, but knowing it would come between them.

"O-M-G, you were right! This furniture is perfect for the space."

Murphy pushed away the morose thoughts, plastered on a smile, and turned to face Kallie. "When will you learn to stop doubting me?"

"About the same time you stop doubting me," Kallie responded with a bright smile and shoved a large bouquet of flowers into his chest. "Come help me get these ready."

The appealing scent of the flowers filled Murphy's nose, and he had to admit, it did smell better than paint and varnish.

He followed Kallie into the kitchen area and set the flowers in the sink. "I know nothing about flowers. I'll have to leave the hard stuff to you."

"Typical man." Kallie rolled her eyes and then laughed. "So have you thought about what you're going to make for dinner?"

"Well...."

"Oh hell no! I am not cooking. You're the one wanting to get laid."

"I don't need to cook to get laid," Murphy countered.

"Typical man," Kallie repeated. She flipped on the water and unwrapped the flowers. "Hand me a pair of scissors."

Murphy dug in the drawer, then handed her a pair.

"See, it's that kind of attitude we need to work on. You don't want to be typical, do you, Murphy?"

Murphy pursed his lips, thinking. Joe was coming up after work to see the place for the first time in a few days. The way Murphy figured it, as soon as he showed Joe the bedroom, neither of them would make it back out to the kitchen. Murphy had kept working at the resort during the day, finishing the renos at night. Five days without so much as a blow job and yeah... dinner wouldn't be high on the list.

Murphy turned to meet Kallie's gaze. "For the record, I am anything but typical. However, for the sake of argument—hypothetically, of course—if I wanted to make a romantic dinner and needed it to be really simple to prepare, what would you suggest?"

Kallie arched a brow. "Hypothetically?"

Murphy nodded, refusing to acknowledge the heat in his cheeks.

"Well, you could always go with a simple Italian pasta dish, a nice bottle of wine, and fresh baked bread."

"And it's something I could make?"

"Sure, well, the pasta anyway. I'd suggest not trying to take on baking bread. I'd pick that up from Tifton's Market. You can get the rest of your dinner supplies there too."

"Where?"

"Tifton's Market. It's two blocks over on Leith Street. I can go with you, if you like, after I finish here."

Murphy watched as Kallie arranged flowers in two separate glass vases. He waited until she was finished before he asked, "How about I go with you, pay for it, and you cook it?" Murphy tried batting his eyes to tempt her. It obviously didn't have the right effect since Kallie burst out laughing.

"Nice try, Romeo, but no." She took one of the arrangements and set it on the nook table, then took the other and set it on the coffee table. "You ready?"

"I can't go right now. The deliverymen still have to bring up the bedroom furniture."

As if on cue, one of the men stepped through the door backward, one end of a box spring in hand.

"Okay, you can help me hang pictures while they work."

"And if I do, will you help me cook?" Murphy asked, hopeful.

Kallie rolled her eyes at him again. "Yes. Now c'mon, we have work to do."

THE SCENT of stewing tomatoes, garlic, and basil mingled with the delicious aroma of grilled chicken filled the small apartment, completely wiping out any trace of the flowery scent prominent when Murphy began cooking. He stirred the sauce, then brought the wooden spoon to his mouth to taste. It tasted even better than it smelled, which was saying something.

Had anyone asked Murphy just one day prior if he could cook, he'd have honestly answered no. He'd tried once again to get Kallie to do it, claiming he would learn more if he was able to observe. She didn't believe him and refused to so much as cut a single pepper or onion. He wasn't quite ready to admit it, at least not to Kallie, but he was now secretly glad she hadn't, because he was really proud of what he'd been able to accomplish and couldn't wait for Joe to try it. He turned the heat on the stove down to warm, covered the pot, and went to set the table.

Five minutes later, everything was prepared, and there was a knock on the door. "Come on in. It's open," Murphy called out.

"Sorry I'm late," Joe said as he walked in.

"Actually you're right on time. Dinner just got done."

Joe sauntered over to Murphy. "It smells great in here." Joe looked over Murphy's shoulder. "Looks good too."

Joe's nearness sent a tingling sensation straight to Murphy's groin. "Did you even notice the new furniture?"

Joe slid both arms around Murphy's waist. "Sorry, I got distracted by this." Joe gave Murphy's crotch a quick squeeze.

"I had my back to you. How did you get distracted by this?" Murphy thrust his hips, pushing his hardening cock against Joe's hand.

"I don't have to see it to be distracted by it."

"Wow, I'll remember that next time. It will save me a ton of work." Murphy chuckled. He turned in Joe's arms and looked up at him. "But since I've been working my fingers to the bone, you're going to wash your hands and sit down."

"Ooh, I love it when you get all alpha on me."

"Be a good boy and eat all your dinner, and I'll show you just how alpha I can get." Murphy gave Joe a shove back, but not before he felt the shiver that went through Joe's body.

Joe was at the sink washing his hands seconds later. Apparently, he liked Murphy's plan. Once Joe took a seat at the table, Murphy dished out pasta and sauce for each of them, set the pot on the table, then went to retrieve the bread and wine.

"Holy shit, Murphy! I didn't know you could cook. This is delicious," Joe said around a mouthful of pasta. "You're just full of surprises, aren't you?"

Murphy grinned. He loved the way Joe's compliments made his stomach flutter pleasantly. He picked up his glass, his chest pushed out in pride. "You don't know the half of it." Murphy sniffed haughtily and took a sip of his wine.

Joe licked his lips and looked at Murphy with heavy-lidded eyes. "I'd like to know. In fact, I'm hoping you show me after dinner."

"Eat up and I'll show you the rest of my talents."

"Mmmm, I can't wait."

Leftovers in the fridge, the last dish dry, Murphy grabbed Joe's hand and pulled him into the main room. "You've already seen the kitchen. What do you think of the living room?"

Joe scanned the room quickly, then settled his gaze back on Murphy. "It's beautiful." Seeing the lust shining in Joe's eyes, Murphy needed little imagination to figure out what Joe was focusing on. It damn sure wasn't the renovation.

Murphy grinned, enjoying the playfulness arcing between them along with the electricity. He spun Joe around and pushed him toward the bathroom. It wasn't really big enough for both of them, so he shoved Joe inside.

"What do you think about the tile we picked out?"

"Love it," Joe murmured, his voice husky. He turned and raked his eyes up and down Murphy's body, and his expression made Murphy think of a predator sizing up his prey. It was Murphy's turn to shudder.

He'd been busting his balls for two weeks and was proud of the work he'd done. It should have bothered him that Joe wasn't taking in a single piece of furniture, built-in shelf, or tile. But it didn't. Not with the way Joe was looking at him and how his shorts were tenting. Joe could check out the place tomorrow.

Still, Murphy was having fun making Joe work for what he wanted.

Once again, he spun out of Joe's reach when he stepped out of the bathroom. Murphy grabbed the doorknob and threw open the door to the bedroom. "This room just needed a little elbow grease and paint."

Joe's lips curved into a wicked smile. "Sounds like this room could use a little more work."

Murphy jerked his head, thinking he had forgotten something, but the room looked perfect. The walls—a deep mocha color with bright white trim—were the perfect backdrop for the dark furniture and pale, plush bedding.

"What do you mean it needs a little more work? I think it looks amazing."

"Almost."

Murphy turned and caught a glimpse of heat flaring in Joe's eyes. In the blink of an eye, Joe had his arms wrapped around Murphy's waist and pushed Murphy onto the bed, making the springs squeak. Then there were no more words as Joe took his mouth in a deep, toe-curling kiss.

We should be talking instead of mauling each other. Yet even as Murphy thought it, he simply couldn't bring himself to stop kissing Joe. There was a good chance that once they talked, Joe might never want to speak to him again.

The whole FF&C thing would be a major obstacle between them, and Murphy knew there was a chance it could destroy things between him and Joe. They had to talk about it and find some sort of common ground. The thing was, it was bound to take them a while to find it, and they'd never get there without more yelling and hurt feelings. He just couldn't deal with that right now.

Enjoy the moment. There's time later to talk.

At least he hoped so. Murphy shoved his worry about the future to the back of his mind. Besides, he convinced himself, even if he wanted to talk, there was no way he could with Joe's tongue down his throat.

Part of Murphy wanted to take it slow, savor every second. But Joe drove him out of his damn mind with lust, and slow and sensual didn't stand a chance. One of Joe's lean legs wound around Murphy's hips, rocking their groins together. The feel of Joe's erection rubbing against his made Murphy's spark of arousal ignite into a raging fire.

Moaning, Murphy slid the hand not buried in Joe's hair up the firm thigh draped across his hip. He got a good handful of Joe's firm ass and squeezed, tearing a ragged groan from Joe's throat.

"I want to fuck you," Murphy growled.

"Best offer I've had all day. Please tell me you thought to add lube to your decorating."

A delicious wave raced up Murphy's spine. "Damn right I did." He disentangled himself from Joe. "Get your clothes off."

"Bossy little shit," Joe complained playfully. But obviously he liked Murphy's plan because he was shoving down his shorts and kicking them off.

"You complaining?"

"Not even a little bit."

"Didn't think so." Murphy shucked his clothes, retrieving the lube and condom he'd stored in his shorts pocket before tossing them and his T-shirt haphazardly. Murphy couldn't help but grin when Joe's gaze landed on his cock, and he swallowed hard. "You're needing a good pounding, aren't you?"

"You know it," Joe groaned and wrapped a fist around his straining prick, pumping it a couple of times.

Murphy pushed up onto one elbow and leaned over until his lips brushed the shell of Joe's ear. "Let go of what's mine, or you'll be earning yourself a good case of blue balls." He licked Joe's earlobe.

Joe's eyes went wide, and he instantly released the hold on his dick. "You wouldn't."

Murphy started to point out that Joe obviously believed him since he'd done what Murphy had told him, but instead he figured Joe needed a reward for his obedience. He shimmied down Joe's body to play with his left nipple with tongue and teeth, teasing the little nub until it was erect, then giving the other nipple the same treatment. Joe arched into Murphy's mouth.

When he finally pulled a shudder from Joe, Murphy lifted his head, leaving Joe's nipple wet and pebbling in the relative cool of the air.

He held up the condom but realized it was all he was holding. "What the hell did I do with that lube?"

Joe dug frantically through the disheveled blankets and after a few seconds held up the battered tube with a crow of triumph. "Lube!"

Murphy snatched it from him with one hand and nudged his thigh with the other. "Spread."

Joe obeyed so fast, Murphy bounced when he hit the mattress between Joe's splayed legs. He laughed. "You're not anxious to get my cock up your ass or anything, are you?"

Joe's response was an arched brow that screamed *Duh*. If that wasn't clue enough, then Joe hooking his arms beneath his knees, pulling them up toward his chest, putting that tight little hole on display, was.

Murphy's gaze zeroed in on Joe's, and he licked his lips. "Jesus, Joe."

"Too slutty?"

"Not unless you do that for everyone."

"Just you."

"Then the only term I'd use to describe it is 'really hot.'"

Bending down, Murphy sucked up a purple mark on the inside of Joe's thigh while he squeezed a generous amount of lube into his hand. He pushed two slippery fingers into Joe's hole, searched out his gland, and rubbed it.

Joe gasped, back arching and hands clutching the covers in a death grip. "Oh damn, Murphy! Right there."

Murphy complied, nudging Joe's sweet spot until Joe was moaning, his body trembling. "God, you're so…." He left the thought unfinished. He twisted and scissored his fingers in Joe's loosening hole. "I can't wait any longer. Please tell me you're ready."

Joe nodded and drew both legs closer to his chest, spreading himself in blatant invitation.

It was an offer Murphy couldn't refuse. He withdrew his fingers, took hold of his cock with one hand, and rested the other on Joe's thigh. He nudged the head of his prick against Joe's hole. Their gazes locked. A single sharp thrust and Murphy was deep inside Joe, and the way Joe's ass clamped down around his cock felt so good that he wanted to howl.

Murphy fell forward, catching his weight on his hands. His eyes fluttered closed, his mouth open. He rocked his hips, eliciting a whimper from Joe. "God, you feel so good."

Joe didn't respond verbally. Instead, he expressed his agreement by draping his legs over Murphy's shoulders and lifting his butt to meet his next thrust. They groaned in stereo, the soft sound nearly drowned out by a slap of skin to skin as Murphy began to pound into Joe.

Joe tangled a hand into Murphy's hair and tugged, the sweet sparks of pain urging Murphy on. He redoubled his efforts, folded Joe in half, and took Joe's mouth in a consuming kiss. Murphy shut his eyes and let the pleasure carry him away.

Not so long ago, going five days—six? Maybe it was six now, he couldn't remember—without sex would've been no big deal. Before Joe came along, Murphy had regularly gone up to two weeks without hooking up with anyone, and once he'd had a dry spell lasting almost three months. However, since hooking up with Joe, he'd become accustomed to sex at least once—and sometimes twice—a day.

Murphy was spoiled, and six days was now way too long to do without, which was probably why he felt his orgasm building inside him after an embarrassingly short time. Judging by Joe's litany of broken moans and the way he was thrashing and jerking, he was having the same problem. It made Murphy feel better to know he wasn't the only one.

"Oh my God." Murphy panted against Joe's lips. "Joe….I'm going to come."

"Do it. Come for me."

Murphy groaned and came, his shaft pulsing deep in Joe's ass, his pleasure intensifying when Joe cried out Murphy's name as he shot all over his chest. Murphy's toes curled hard as Joe's untouched cock splattered them both with what had to be almost a week's worth of semen.

Dipping his head, Murphy collected a quick kiss before shrugging Joe's legs off his shoulders and collapsing onto Joe's chest. His softened cock slipped from Joe's hole.

Joe squeaked, and Murphy laughed. "Man, I seriously needed that."

"Me too." Joe wrapped both arms around Murphy. "Don't make me wait that long again, eh?"

Murphy buried his face against the side of Joe's neck, breathing harshly. Reality came rushing back as he floated down from his orgasmic bliss. He didn't want to deal with the guilt and all the other emotions rushing through him.

"We're going to have to talk eventually," Murphy whispered, but he knew Joe wouldn't be able to make out what he was saying. He truly was a coward.

They fell silent. Thunder rolled in the distance as a storm moved in.

Obviously Joe *had* heard him because after a few moments he said, "I don't want to talk right now, do you?"

"Nope." Murphy tightened his grip on Joe.

"Cuddle now. Talk later."

Murphy chuckled. "I don't cuddle." However, even as he protested, he pulled Joe closer still.

"Mmmhmm."

Murphy ignored the skepticism he heard from Joe because he was warm and sleepy and fading fast. He shifted, burrowing his face into Joe's throat. A faint snore escaped him, causing him to jerk, but then Joe caressed his cheek, easing him back to sleep.

Chapter Fourteen

KALLIE STOOD behind the counter at Kaffeinate, her eyes as wide as saucers. "You have to tell him, Murphy."

Murphy hung his head, no longer able to meet Kallie's disapproving gaze. "I know, and I'd planned on telling him last night, but...." Murphy waved his hand, then shrugged. "One thing led to another and...." *I fucked his brains out.* "Well, we just didn't get around to talking about it."

"You have to stop thinking with your little head and be honest with him. You owe him that."

The sharpness in Kallie's voice made Murphy frown at her. "You don't think I know that?"

"Then do—"

"It's not that goddamn easy! He's going to freak out, may never speak to me again, and then what?"

"That is something you're going to have to take a chance on. The one thing Joe prides himself on is his honesty, and he demands that from those he cares about."

Nodding, Murphy stirred his coffee, watching the dark liquid swirl around in his cup rather than having to look at the disappointment in Kallie's eyes. *Dammit.* He already knew the truth without Kallie pointing it out. It was unfair to keep it from Joe, but at the end of the day, it was simply a job, a damn good-paying job. Plus, he was learning things from George and Danny, the HVAR supervisor at Calm Winds Resort. FF&C might own the property, but other than their signature on his paychecks, Murphy had nothing to do with the company.

"So are you going to tell him? He has a right to know," Kallie urged.

Murphy managed a small smile, even as his emotions were waging war in his head and heart. "I'll tell him."

Kallie laid a hand on Murphy's shoulder. "Joe may not like what you have to say, but he's a reasonable man. Explain it to him the way you did me, because you're right about Calm Winds. The resort is here to stay whether we like it or not. Working on a couple air conditioners for an honest wage isn't going to make a difference in the big scheme of things. He will, however, respect your honesty."

"You're right. I would have respected your honesty."

Murphy spun around to find Joe standing behind them, his arms crossed over his chest and his lips pressed tightly together.

Murphy's chest tightened and bile rose up into his throat. He could tell by the cold fury in Joe's eyes that he'd heard enough of the conversation to know Murphy had been keeping things from him.

"Joe...." Joe turned and started to walk away. Murphy jumped up and grabbed Joe's arm before he got more than a few feet. "Joe, wait."

Joe stopped but didn't turn around. "Let go," he responded, his voice tight.

"Joe, please," Murphy implored. "Just let me explain."

JOE CLOSED his eyes and took a couple of deep breaths. He could not talk to Murphy right now. He was too angry and too hurt. If they tried to talk it out now, Joe would end up saying something he'd regret. He knew better than to speak in anger, because he'd no doubt regret it and there would be no way to take it back.

"Not now," Joe said, opening his eyes and squaring his shoulders. "I can't talk to you right now. I need some time."

Murphy remained silent behind him, and he began to worry that Murphy wasn't going to let him go. Fury that wanted so badly to be released bubbled up, but Joe swallowed it down. As calmly as he could muster, he tugged his arm loose from Murphy's grip. To his relief, Murphy's hand opened and Joe was free.

"Can we please talk later?" Murphy asked, sounding desperate and so incredibly sad, Joe nearly turned around. But he couldn't. Not now.

Nodding, Joe walked away without looking back. Rather than seeking out the privacy and security of his office, he headed to the front door and out into the humid summer morning. Joe ignored those who waved or greeted him, his head down and steps heavy as he stomped along the sidewalk. He hadn't been this pissed in... hell, he couldn't remember the last time he'd been this furious. The fact that Murphy had told Kallie he was working for Fields, Fields, and Cohen before he'd told Joe was intolerable. Even more infuriating, Murphy felt he couldn't tell Joe the truth, yet he could share it with Kallie. It truly cut him to the core.

Joe knew he had no right to tell Murphy what to do or where he could or couldn't work. His anger went well beyond something so trivial. What he couldn't accept or understand at all was the fact that Murphy obviously didn't think enough of him to tell him the truth. He was surprised by how much that hurt.

Each step he took, he warred between wanting to scream and hit something and wanting to curl up in a ball and cry. His composure hung by a very thin thread, and he didn't think he could hold himself together much longer. Luckily, Joe made it back to his bungalow without completely losing it. Once inside, he kicked the door shut so hard the walls shook, slumped onto the couch, and hung his head in his hands.

Anger lost the battle in the wake of the incredible sadness that enveloped him. A hollow ache lodged itself deep in his chest. *Why couldn't he tell me? What is it about me that he couldn't trust me with the truth?*

"Why, Murphy?" he whispered to the empty room. He pressed the heels of his palms against his eyes in an attempt to hold back the tears that threatened.

How long he sat there in that miserable state, he didn't know. He was simply thankful when he realized he didn't really feel anything except numb. Sighing, Joe opened his eyes and stared at threadbare carpet under his feet. He had no idea what to do now. Part of him wanted to find Murphy and give him a chance to explain. There had to be a reason Murphy hadn't felt he could talk to Joe about this. Murphy obviously trusted Kallie, so was it something about Joe that Murphy didn't feel the same comfort level?

Before Joe could get sucked back into another round of emotional battleship, someone pounded on the door. He groaned. There was only one person it could possibly be, and Joe wasn't at all sure he was ready to face him.

"Joe? Let me in, okay?"

Hearing Murphy's voice made Joe's chest tighten painfully. He ran both hands through his hair. Maybe if he didn't answer, Murphy would give up and go away.

"Come on, Joe, open the door." The doorknob rattled. "Give me a chance to explain, to apologize." After a long silence, Murphy knocked on the door again. "Please, Joe. Give me the chance to apologize, and if you never want to speak to me again, I'll leave you alone. I promise."

Joe squeezed his eyes shut and blew out a heavy breath. The sadness slammed back into him full force with the thought of Murphy walking away and Joe never seeing him again.

"Please. Give me five minutes."

Joe sighed. Why did Murphy have to sound so lost? He had to know there was no way Joe could leave him standing out there like a damn stray puppy.

Steeling himself, Joe stood, crossed the few feet to the door, and flung it open. "Okay. Talk."

Murphy not only sounded like a lost puppy but looked like one too. His shoulders slumped and he wrung his hands as he shifted from foot to foot. "You have to believe me, Joe. I'm so sorry you had to hear it like that. I was going to tell you, I swear to God I was."

It took every ounce of Joe's strength to keep from grabbing Murphy and pulling him into a tight embrace. It amazed Joe how quickly Murphy could melt him and wipe out the last traces of Joe's anger. Joe was able to resist the urge, but he couldn't think with Murphy so close, and he desperately needed to keep his wits about him right now.

"Why didn't you tell me about taking the job with Fields, Fields, and Cohen?" Joe asked, holding Murphy's gaze.

"I knew you'd be mad." Murphy continued to fidget and worried his bottom lip with his teeth. "Are you going to let me come in?"

Joe took a step back and gestured. Once Murphy was in, Joe shut the door, then returned to his position on the couch and rubbed both hands over his face. "I need to know why you felt you could trust Kallie with this information and not me. I mean, seriously, Murphy, what am I supposed to think about that?"

"That I'm an idiot?" Murphy sat on the coffee table and laid a hand on Joe's knee. "I knew you'd be mad, and so I told Kallie, asking her advice. She told me to tell you, that you might understand as long as I was honest. I went to her first because I didn't want to ruin things between us, but it seems like I did that anyway."

"You know how I feel about them," Joe pointed out, unable to keep the sadness out of his voice.

"I know, but I really didn't get a chance to explain my position."

Joe arched a brow in disbelief.

Murphy quickly added, "You were instantly mad, like visibly shaking the moment you heard the name Fields, Fields, and Cohen. I didn't want to make it worse. I hated seeing you like that."

"Murphy, after knowing how I feel, how can you say that? Of course you'd make it worse by taking money from those cheating, stealing bastards."

"I know you're mad about what they tried to do to you and the others on your block. But Seaside resorts don't have any injunctions or lawsuits pending. I'm simply working for an established resort, and it's a good job, with good pay. Plus, I'm learning a lot. FF&C may own the property, but other than their signature on the paychecks, I have nothing to do with the company. Mr. Barton thought I would get some great experience and it's only temporary."

Joe pursed his lips. "Only to take money from the devil once again."

Murphy sat back and glared at Joe. "Did you not hear a single thing I just said?"

"Yeah, I heard you. Regardless that I told you not to, you went behind my back and went to work for those... those...." Joe threw up his hands in frustration.

Murphy went rigid, his expression hard. "What did you just say?"

"You heard me."

"Yeah, I heard you. I just can't believe you said that to me. You *told* me not to take the job?" Murphy stood, towering over him, his face an angry shade of red. "Who the hell are you to tell me what I can and can't do?"

Shocked, Joe stared. "You asked my opinion!"

"The hell I did," Murphy spat. Spinning on his heel, he crossed to the door.

Joe jumped to his feet and cut Murphy off. He stood between Murphy and the door and used his height to look down his nose at Murphy. "Where the hell do you think you are going?"

"Oh, what, you're going to tell me when I can leave and where to go? Maybe you can teach me a few tricks while you're at it, like sit, stay, roll over!" Murphy pressed his hands to Joe's chest and shoved him back. "And stop trying to intimidate me with your height. I have done some verbal sparring with men a hell of a lot scarier than you, and I wasn't afraid."

"I didn't mean you had to ask permission. I was asking you where you were going."

"None of your business. Now get out of my way," Murphy demanded. His chest pushed out, nose flaring as he breathed harshly.

"Knock it off. Let's talk this out like two rational adults."

"Get. Out. Of. My. Way," Murphy ground out.

Joe crossed his arms over his chest and refused to step out of the way.

"Move."

Joe shook his head. "No. We need to talk about this and come to some kind of resolution."

Murphy obviously wasn't about to talk because he planted his hand on Joe's hip and easily shoved Joe out of the way. Joe staggered, catching himself on the wall before he landed on his ass. Before Joe could react, Murphy snatched the door open and was gone.

Joe briefly thought about chasing after him. Ugh! Why in the hell did Murphy have to be so goddamn stubborn? Why did Joe care where Murphy worked? Had he seriously tried to tell Murphy what to do? When had Murphy become so damned important to him that he'd start a fight over where he worked? When had Joe taken his feelings for Murphy out of the bedroom and begun viewing him as potential boyfriend material?

Probably about the time you fell in love with him.

Startled, Joe closed the door and leaned heavily against it. Did he really love Murphy?

He thought about it and realized he did.

Joe hung his head in shame. "Great, way to run off the man you love, asshole."

REGARDLESS THAT I told you not to.

Joe's statement kept playing over and over in Murphy's head. Each time he wanted to scream or stomp or hit something. Well, he was stomping down the street, each step hard and angry. He had to let it out somehow, or he'd take it out on the unsuspecting people he passed. How dare Joe think he could tell him what he could and couldn't do! It wasn't Joe paying his bills, feeding him, or clothing him. It certainly wasn't Joe's place to tell Murphy to abandon his dreams simply because he didn't like Murphy's employer—temporary employer, no less.

He had the right to be pissed. It was Joe who was in the wrong. However, Murphy certainly was dealing with his own healthy dose of guilt. It bothered him that he hadn't been honest with Joe. He'd planned on telling Joe, had thought he'd had a good excuse, but now…. He wasn't so sure. The hurt in Joe's eyes as he pointed out that Murphy had been able to trust Kallie with the truth, but not Joe, had dug through the anger and ripped at his heart. That tidbit was bothering him the most.

Why in the hell couldn't he hold on to his anger? He was entitled to his outrage at Joe's statement. Wasn't he?

Problem was, the harder he tried to blame Joe for everything, the more Murphy choked on his anger as the contrition rose like bile.

Murphy stopped dead in his tracks. Something slammed into him and pitched him forward. At the last second, he got his feet beneath him before he fell flat on his face. He turned around to see the horrified expression of a young girl, her cheeks bright red.

"I'm so sorry," she said. "I didn't expect you to stop like that. Are you okay?" Another young girl next to her had her hand over her mouth, and Murphy could tell she was fighting to keep her laughter in.

"I'm fine," he assured her. He nodded to her friend. "Go ahead and laugh. I deserve it for being such a putz."

That was all it took. She broke out in a fit of giggles. Murphy winked at the girl who had bumped into him. "Too bad you didn't knock me on my butt. Someone needs to."

She gave him a strange look, and then she and the giggling friend hurried away. Murphy leaned against a wall, out of the way of the people walking down the sidewalk. Regardless of what he'd said, it wasn't his ass that needed the abuse—but he did need some sense knocked into him. He'd been struggling with so many conflicting emotions, and it was really quite simple. Joe had strolled right past all Murphy's reasons for not wanting anyone to get too close. Joe ignored them all and firmly attached himself to Murphy's heart. He hadn't been looking for it, had fought it, but it didn't change the facts. He was… no, he *had* fallen for Joe, and Joe's opinions did matter, because Joe mattered.

Chapter Fifteen

"No, he hasn't come in, called, or messaged me in the last ten minutes since the last time you called," Kallie announced in an irritated tone as soon as she picked up.

Goddammit, Murphy. Where in the hell are you? Joe cleared his throat. "I'm worried. Where in the hell is he?"

"Like I'm supposed to know. He's probably somewhere cooling down. Now will you stop calling me, or better yet, get your butt out here and help? We're swamped."

"Yeah, I'll be out in a minute." He set the phone into the cradle and dropped his head into his hands. Murphy wouldn't call him back. He'd been trying to get ahold of the man for the past twenty-four hours. He'd left dozens of messages on voicemail and an untold number of texts, begging Murphy to at least let him know that he was okay. No such luck.

Raising his head, Joe glanced at the clock on the wall of his office—nine fifteen. Jesus, no wonder Kallie was irked with him. It was the height of rush hour in the shop. He swore under his breath. Maybe if he immersed himself in work, he wouldn't have time to think about Murphy. It sounded good but didn't mean shit. He'd thought of little else since yesterday morning. Truth be told, he'd thought of little else since meeting the man.

And you ran him off with your possessive, neurotic ways. Way to go, dipshit.

Joe let out a pent-up breath. What the hell was wrong with him? He had no right to tell Murphy where he could or couldn't work. Hell, he didn't have the right to tell Murphy anything. Suggest, maybe, but demand? No.

So now, not only was he unbelievably sad because of his fight with Murphy, he was dealing with a healthy dose of guilt. In fact, guilty was the understatement of the century. It had taken all but the slam of his door for Joe's anger to fade and, in its wake, a nearly crippling feeling of remorse. He had to apologize, beg even, but he could do neither if Murphy refused to talk to him.

Sighing, Joe pushed out of his chair, pulled up his big-boy panties, and headed out to the café. Nothing he could do about it at the moment.

Kaffeinate was insane. A tour bus full of senior citizens was making a pit stop on their way to the casino. It was nuts, but Joe was thankful for the distraction. Not that he didn't keep checking his cell phone or hoping each time the bell rang over the door that it would be Murphy who was walking through.

They'd waved to the last of the day-trippers when Joe's phone vibrated. Fishing the cell out of the pocket of his cargo shorts, he checked the display and nearly had a heart attack when he saw Murphy's number.

He flipped the phone open and pressed it to his ear. "Murphy?"

"Yeah. Um. Hi."

The sound of Murphy's voice set Joe's insides churning. "Hi. I've been trying to get ahold of you."

An awkward, thankfully short silence followed before Murphy answered. "I know. Sorry I haven't called you back before. I guess I needed time to cool down."

Kallie shooed Joe and mouthed *I got this*. Joe rushed to his office and slumped in his chair.

"Are you there?"

"Yes, I'm here. I'm so sorry, Murphy. I was way out of line yesterday morning. I have no excuse for my behavior. I had no right."

There was a heartbeat of quiet on the other end. "I'm sorry too. I shouldn't have run. I should have stayed and worked this out."

"I want to work this out, Murphy. I…." Joe swallowed around the swell of emotion lodged in his throat. "I miss you."

"Yeah, I miss you too. You think we can get past this?"

"I know we can." Switching his phone to his left ear, Joe picked up a pen and tapped it on his desk. "Can we meet? I can come to you or you can come here. Whichever is fine with me."

"I can't. I'm at work and only have a minute to talk." Murphy sighed. "How about after work?"

Joe gritted his teeth and pushed away the anger that tried to bubble up. He was going to have to get used to Murphy working for FF&C because he damn sure wasn't going to give Murphy up.

"I have to meet the tile installer at the beach house at five. I can cancel or you could come over or…. Just tell me when and where and I'll be there."

"I'll come over, say nine?"

Joe wanted to protest. He didn't want to wait that long. Hell, he wanted to rush out the door and go find him right now. Instead he responded, "I'll be there. I can't wait to see you."

"You don't know how happy that makes me." Murphy laughed softly. "I've gotta run. See you tonight."

"Wait a minute, I—"

"I'm sorry, but I really have to go. My boss is eyeballing me."

"But—"

"We'll talk tonight. Bye."

The line went dead. Joe shut down his phone and set it on the desk with a huge smile on his face. "Well, that went well."

A knock sounded on the door. Joe sighed. "Come in."

The door opened, and Kallie's smiling face popped through the gap. "Hey, how did your convo go? Good, I hope."

Joe pursed his lips and sat back in his chair. "When did you get so interested in my love life?"

"Pfft. I've always been interested in your love life, but even more so since you've met Murphy. I like him."

"Yeah, I like him too." Joe gave her a sly smile.

Kallie waved a dismissive hand and entered the office. She didn't wait to be invited, simply took the chair across from Joe and gave him an expectant look. "I've seen you in 'like,'" she reminded him. "This goes way deeper than simple 'like.' Did you tell him?"

Joe arched a brow. "Tell him what?"

He chuckled at the exasperated expression on her face. After he told her what had happened between him and Murphy, she hadn't been too happy with him. She thought he deserved a slap upside the head for being such an idiot. Actually, she'd threatened that if Joe didn't apologize and make things right with Murphy, she'd go on strike. Again with the women in his life threatening bodily harm and blackmail. He was beginning to see a pattern but wasn't quite ready to admit they were right. Although secretly he was beginning to believe they usually were.

"No, he only had a second to talk. He's coming over later tonight," Joe said, purposely keeping it vague.

She grinned. "But you're going to, aren't you?"

Joe pushed his chair back and stood. "Don't you have work to do or something?"

Kallie jumped up and clapped. "I knew it," she squealed.

Joe cocked his head. "Okay, I have no idea why you're so excited about going back to work. I swear, I'll never understand women."

"You're not supposed to understand. It's part of our charm." She went up on tiptoe and pecked his cheek before heading out the door. Joe stared at the empty space and scratched his head. Then Kallie appeared again. "And don't you chicken out. I know he loves you too."

Joe grabbed the cushion from his chair and threw it at her. He missed—the little vixen was far too quick. Her laughter trailed with her down the hall.

MURPHY PLACED his hands on either side of the small opening in the ceiling and pulled himself up. Careful to stay on the wooden planks, he crawled along toward the hole in the ductwork the robotic camera had discovered earlier. He was the newbie, so of course he got the shit jobs, but he didn't mind, especially this morning. His fight with Joe, followed by the realization that he cared about the man, had thrown his mind and emotions into turmoil. The last twenty-four hours had been pure agony, and he'd barely slept a wink. He was tired, but since talking to Joe, he was a happy man. They were talking again, Joe apologized, and tonight he'd be sleeping in Joe's bed. Soon, everything in Murphy's world would be right again.

As it turned out, Murphy's happiness faltered when Jake, the night foreman, informed him he'd be working a double, but it couldn't erase it.

A quick call to Joe, letting him know he'd be late, had turned his frown upside down when Joe had replied, "Just come on in when you get here. I'll be waiting."

It was well after midnight by the time he made it to Joe's place. Murphy laughed softly when just the sight of the outside light being left on made him smile. Quietly, in case Joe had fallen asleep, Murphy let himself in the unlocked front door. He took off his boots and set them aside. Just past the foyer, Murphy's smile grew, and he leaned against the entryway and enjoyed the sight before him for a moment. Joe was sitting on the couch with one foot tucked beneath him and his head on the padded arm. His eyes were closed, mouth open and slack with sleep. He looked so peaceful Murphy hated to wake him up, but the urge to touch was too great. He walked over to Joe and gently brushed a stray strand of hair from his brow, then slid his fingertips softly along Joe's cheek. Joe's brow furrowed. His eyes fluttered open and focused on Murphy's face.

The corners of Joe's mouth curled up in a sleepy smile. "Hi."

"Hi. Sorry I'm late."

"You're right on time."

They stared at each other, and suddenly the moment Murphy'd been looking forward to all day seemed awkward. "Um. So. Yeah…. How have you been?" *Oh, great babbling, you idiot.* Christ, he'd never felt so strange and tongue-tied in his life.

Thankfully, Joe knew exactly what to say. "I don't know about you, but I could use a hug."

Joe opened his arms, and Murphy happily dropped to his knees between Joe's thighs and accepted the embrace. For long moments they clung to each other, no words needed, letting their caressing and soothing hands speak for themselves. Murphy started to melt into Joe, wanting nothing more than to grab him and take him to bed, show him with his body how happy he was to see him and how much he'd missed him. He reluctantly pulled back and looked up at Joe, whose eyes were as bloodshot as Murphy's felt.

"We seriously need to talk."

Joe sighed. "I know, but God, I'm tired. I didn't get much sleep last night."

Murphy nodded. "I know the feeling."

Joe laid his hand against Murphy's cheek. "Were you as miserable as I was?"

Murphy started to answer, but the words were cut off by a yawn.

Joe tilted Murphy's head back and planted a soft kiss on his lips. "My brain is mush, and you look as tired as I feel. How about you get up here and cuddle me for a couple of hours, and then I promise we'll talk."

He kissed Murphy again, deeper this time, until Murphy felt the power of Joe's passion right in the center of his chest and a tingling sensation tickled along his spine. His dick made a gallant effort to fill, but he was simply too exhausted.

With great effort, Murphy drew away. "I don't cuddle. But if you take me to bed, I'll let you hug me while I sleep."

Joe gave him a crooked smile. "I can't wait to get you in bed. I think I may even be able to muster up enough energy for a quickie."

"Uh-huh," Murphy said skeptically as he got to his feet. He held out a hand and helped Joe stand. He swayed a little, but Murphy wrapped an arm around his waist to steady him. "You can do me if you can get it up."

"Deal."

It was no surprise that neither of them lasted longer than it took to brush their teeth, undress, and crawl between the sheets. Joe planted a sweet kiss on Murphy's lips, then snuggled against his chest. Joe fell asleep clutching Murphy to him like an oversized teddy bear. Unlike Murphy, Joe was a major snuggler.

Murphy was simply Joe's sleeping aid, and truth be told, he frickin' loved it.

Chapter Sixteen

IN HIS warm cocoon, eyes still closed, Murphy reached out for Joe and frowned when he found nothing but cold sheets. He sat up, blinking until his eyes adjusted to the lack of light. Joe wasn't in the room, but the scent of bacon cooking clued Murphy in as to where the object of his desire was. He threw off the covers and shuffled sleepily to the bathroom. He took care of his morning business, washed his face and hands, and then brushed his teeth. When he straightened, he winced when he caught his reflection. The lack of sleep and long work hours were still evident in the form of dark circles beneath his bloodshot eyes. He looked like hell.

It was only after he pulled on his clothes and checked his cell phone that he realized how damn early it was. Who in the hell got up at four in the morning and cooked breakfast? He headed to the kitchen to find Joe standing at the stove, his lean hips swaying to something he was singing. Murphy couldn't make out the words and didn't recognize the tune but knew it was an upbeat song by the rhythm of Joe's movements and the way he was bobbing his head.

"That's just wrong," Murphy pointed out.

Joe spun around, a spatula in hand and a huge smile on his face. "Morning, sunshine. What's just wrong?"

"For any human being to be that goddamn chipper this early in the morning," Murphy grumbled.

"You sound like you could use a cup of coffee."

"You have no idea," Murphy responded. His gaze narrowed in on the full pot, and he headed toward it.

"I think this is one of the best times of the day. My little neck of the woods is quiet. Nothing but birds and waves for company. No hustle and bustle, very little noise—it's like this beautiful calm before the storm of humanity."

Murphy poured a cup, brought it to his mouth, and blew on the steaming brew. "If you're not up to company, I can head out, but not until I've had at least one cup."

"I wasn't talking about you, silly man. I like having you here." Joe pointed his spatula toward the coffeepot. "Mind pouring me a cup?"

"Oh, sorry. It's a little too early for my manners."

"Stick around me long enough and I'll make a morning person out of ya."

A pleasant fluttering sensation tickled Murphy's belly. He liked the idea of "sticking around," but he seriously doubted he'd ever become a lover of mornings before sunrise. Murphy didn't respond. Instead, he took the time as he poured Joe a cup to muse over the feelings that were quickly taking hold of him where it came to Joe.

Chapter Seventeen

"MORNING, MURPHY," George greeted. His voice was cheery as always, but he looked tired. The lines in his face were more pronounced, and dark bags hung under his eyes.

"Morning. Everything okay?" Murphy asked with true concern.

"I'm fine, just feeling my age this morning. I tell you, son, don't get old. It's a trap, I tell you."

"I've heard that. Tied one on last night, did you?"

"I wish. My daughter popped out a kid last night."

"Hey! Congrats, Grandpa." Murphy patted George on the back. "Everyone doing okay?"

"Much better than my old and dragging ass."

"Pfft, you're not old. What are you, like forty-five?"

"Fifty-seven."

Murphy was shocked. He would never have guessed George was that old. Sure, he had plenty of wrinkles on his weatherworn face. But he'd assumed it was premature aging from the many hours working and playing under the harsh Florida sun. Other than that, the guy was in better shape than most twenty-year-olds Murphy knew. George's arms were strong, the muscles well-defined. Murphy had never seen George without his shirt, but he was sure the man was sporting a six-pack beneath.

"Okay, Grandpa, you can take it easy today," Murphy teased good-heartedly. "I'll take up the slack."

"Damn right you will. The air isn't flowing properly on the top floor. I need you to go through the ductwork and see if you can find any blockages or leaks."

Murphy groaned. He'd been in that large maze of galvanized tin. When the air wasn't on, the maze was stifling hot.

"Aww, don't look so upset. Tell you what, I'll buy you a beer after work."

Murphy picked up his tool belt from the seat of the van and secured it around his waist. "Sounds good to me, but I'd have figured you'd be wanting to get to the hospital."

"She had one of those all-natural, all-organic homebirths." George wrinkled his nose. "I'm telling you, Murphy, some things can never be unseen."

"From the look on your face, I take it, it wasn't a pleasant experience."

"That wasn't anything for a man to witness, especially a father." George shook his head. "Now get to work. Get it done quickly and we'll take an early lunch."

"You're talking my language, old man." Murphy chuckled.

After assuring the system was, in fact, turned off, Murphy donned his paper suit, complete with matching cap and booties. The temperature instantly increased dramatically. The suit was to protect anyone from contaminating the air system, but the creature sure as hell didn't appear to care about the person having to wear it. The material didn't breathe, and Murphy was sweating before doing a lick of work.

He stared up at the latch. *Better get this over with.* He set his equipment in the duct and then pulled himself up through the access panel. He switched on the light he'd secured around his forehead and, on his hands and knees, made his way through the tunnels, inspecting each joint and panel. The heat was insufferable, but Murphy forced himself to move, keeping his eye on the prize. It wasn't for pride in workmanship, nor for the paycheck, but for the prospect of an ice-cold beer when the job was done.

He really had taken Doc's comment to heart. It was the little things in life that made one happy. With any luck it would be more than one, and if Murphy was really lucky, he'd be able to convince George to bugger off the rest of the workday.

It seemed to take an excruciatingly long time but was in all actuality less than an hour before Murphy finally found the problem. An entire seam had come unriveted and left a gaping hole, allowing the cool air to drift into the rafters above. Voices rose from the office below, rising to Murphy's ear from the grate in muffled tones.

It was probably unethical and totally wrong, but Murphy couldn't resist the temptation. Quietly, he stretched out and positioned himself so he could peer down into the office.

Sitting behind an ornately carved wooden desk sat a middle-aged man, his gut so large the button of his suit coat looked as if it would pop at any moment. Large floppy jowls hung from his cleanly shaved and bright red face. He pounded his portly fist against the desk as he growled something Murphy couldn't make out. The man reminded Murphy of a *Looney Tunes* character. The only thing missing was a fat stogie hanging from the side of his mouth. On the other side of the desk sat a cowering man who looked like an old-fashioned bookkeeper, right down to the wire-rimmed spectacles that sat precariously on the tip of his long slender nose. Whatever the big man was saying, it was scaring the smaller man. He looked like he was about to shit himself.

Murphy laid his ear against the grate and strained to hear the conversation. Luckily, Porky Man raised his voice unknowingly, facilitating Murphy's eavesdropping.

Porky Man pointed one meaty finger at Bookkeeper. "I'm getting sick and tired of hearing you tell me you can't. I suggest you find a way or I will bury you. Is that understood?"

"Yes… yes… sir… but—"

"I don't want to hear any buts," Porky Man roared. "I want that block."

"I understand that, sir. But this historical society—"

"I don't give a shit about them. Find a way around it. I don't care if you have to burn the coffee shop, the general store—hell, burn the entire city block to the ground. I want it. Is that understood?" The phone rang. Porky Man laid his hand on top of the receiver, but before picking it up, he pointed at Bookkeeper again. "Now get out of my office and don't come back until it's done."

"Yes, sir. I'll take care of it." Bookkeeper got to his feet and scurried out of Murphy's vision, and a second later Murphy heard the distinct sound of a door opening and closing.

Porky Man picked up the phone and sat back in his leather chair. "This is Mr. Fields."

Murphy's eyes went wide. So that was Mr. Fields. No wonder he was rich. He was a ruthless prick. Murphy's eyes went wider still, and his heart stopped. Historical society? Burn it down? *Holy Shit.* Mr. Fields was talking about Joe's block. The son of a bitch planned to get his hands on Kaffeinate and the rest of the businesses surrounding it.

Mr. Fields continued to talk on the phone, but he'd lowered his voice and Murphy couldn't hear what was being said.

I have to tell Joe.

Murphy inched his way slowly away from the grate, careful not to make a noise. His first instinct was to get to Joe, job be damned. But that was the adrenaline talking. Nothing was going to happen in the next hour or two. Besides, what would he tell George? No, he'd finish the repair and take George up on that early lunch offer. As soon as he was away from the resort, he'd call Joe. Plus, what the hell was he supposed to say? That he was spying on the head of a large and powerful corporation? Murphy had no proof, and even if he did, he was sure they would be after him as soon as they discovered he'd been sent to work in the ductwork above the corporate offices. No, he had to come up with a plan. He'd act like everything was normal, and then the first chance he got, he'd tell Joe what he'd overheard. He had to keep his name out of it. More importantly, today would be the last day he'd set foot in any building owned and operated by Fields, Fields, and Cohen. Paycheck be damned. He wouldn't work for the corrupt bastards.

Quietly, Murphy moved a considerable distance from the grate, nearly back to the starting point. This time he made sure to make enough noise so anyone below could hear him. He started whistling for good measure. How he made the repair, Murphy wasn't sure. His mind was racing, and he had a hard time breathing, let alone focusing on tin and rivets. Somehow he managed. By eleven, two and a half hours after he began, Murphy was heading out the door. He found George sitting in the passenger seat of the BMC van, his head tipped back, mouth open and eyes closed. Poor guy really had a rough night.

Murphy gently shook George's shoulder. "George. You ready for that beer?"

George jerked upright, looking panicked for a brief moment. Then he rubbed his eyes. "Sorry, must have dozed off. Did you find the problem?"

"Understandable," Murphy replied. He opened the sliding door and loaded up his equipment. "Yeah. One of the sections of ductwork must not have been riveted properly. Big gaping hole. All fixed now. So, I ask again, you ready for that beer?" Murphy slid the door closed.

"That and some greasy bar food."

"Like music to my ears." He patted George's arm. "Buckle up. I'll drive."

Murphy fired up the van and pulled out of the parking lot, continuously checking the rearview mirror. It was ridiculous; he doubted Mr. Fields knew he'd been overheard. Still, the strange sensation stuck with Murphy well after he'd left the resort behind. It took everything in him not to race to Joe's place.

Deep breath, dude. You're losing it.

This time he listened to the voice in his head. He couldn't afford to go off half-cocked and bring suspicion on him. If Mr. Fields had no qualms about burning down an entire city block, he surely wouldn't allow some factory worker from Michigan with only a few bucks to his name bring him down.

"Where do you want to eat?" Murphy asked George, surprised that his voice was even, considering the panic running rampant inside him.

"How about the Shack down on Western Street? They have cold beer, fresh seafood, and they're cheap."

"The Shack it is." Murphy hadn't eaten there before but had passed by it, and the crew talked about it often.

The place wasn't anything special, a typical beachfront bar with the tacky ocean décor that appealed to the tourists. "Hi, George," a cheery waitress greeted as she passed with a large tray weighted down with food.

"Hi, sweetie," George responded with a large smile.

Much to Murphy's surprise, his stomach growled when he got a whiff of fried fish and garlic that trailed behind the waitress. Murphy followed George to the bar and took a seat next to him.

"They have the best fried grouper in the state," George informed him.

"Best fried grouper in the nation," the bartender amended. He set down a cocktail napkin in front of Murphy and George. He pointed at George. "Bud Lite"—then pointed at Murphy—"and for you?"

"Guinness Extra Stout if you have it."

"Do I have it." The bartender rolled his eyes.

"Don't mind Victor. He likes to brag, but the fish really is that good."

Victor returned with their beers, and Murphy and George both ordered the grouper. "I'm going to hit the john before lunch. Be right back."

George nodded around his mug.

The instant the door was closed and locked, Murphy pulled out his cell phone and dialed Joe. It went straight to voicemail.

"You've reached Joe. I can't take your call right now, but if you'd like to leave a message, I'll get back to you as soon as possible."

Murphy wasn't about to tell Joe what he'd learned over a message. When the phone beeped, Murphy said, "It's Murphy. Call me when you get a chance." He then added, "It's important."

He ended the call and returned the phone to his pocket. It was probably just as well, because seriously, he wasn't about to get into it on the phone. This was a conversation better to have face-to-face. Then Joe could see the sincerity in Murphy's eyes when he apologized for being a dick, for doubting Joe, and, more importantly, for not trusting him.

Murphy washed his hands and ran his fingers through his tousled hair. It had been such a short time since he'd left Michigan, and already Murphy barely recognized the man staring back at him from the mirror. Strange, that.

It wasn't as if he was running from anything or disliked the man he'd been in Michigan. There was the irritation of his ex, but their breakup hadn't been traumatic for either of them. He had a great family, amazing friends, a good life. Still, as far back as he could remember, he'd dreamed of leaving Michigan. It ran deeper than simply his dislike of the cold winters. He wasn't sure what it was, but the desire had been there all the same.

And there he was, looking like a complete stranger, living in Florida, his dream come true. Until this. Now, he was once again without a job, and it looked as if his dream was going to be a very, very short one.

God, he could be so melodramatic sometimes.

He flipped off his reflection and headed out to rejoin George. He was surprised to find his food waiting for him. He slid into his stool. "Damn, that was fast."

"Damn, I was planning on eating yours," George commented around a big mouthful of fish.

Murphy pulled his plate out of George's reach. "The hell you say." He picked off a piece of fish and popped it in his mouth. It was amazingly delicious. He'd have sworn only a short time ago that he wouldn't have been able to eat with the way his gut was flip-flopping, but he was suddenly famished and devoured his fish, coleslaw, and every last fry. He swiped his napkin over his mouth, then dropped it on his empty plate.

"I told you it was good. The cherry on top, so to speak, is their key lime pie."

Murphy shook his head and sat back in his chair with a satisfied grin and patted his gut. "No way I could eat another bite."

"Well, you don't mind waiting till I have mine, do ya?"

"Hell no, I don't mind. Take all the time you need. The longer we're here means the less time we have to work."

George waved Victor over. "We're not going back. I'm taking a nap and you can do whatever it is you do when you're not working."

He ordered his dessert, and Murphy ordered another beer. He waited until Victor moved out of earshot before he turned to George. "Can I ask you something?"

"Sure."

"What do you know about Fields, Fields, and Cohen?"

"I know they are some wealthy SOBs. Own a good chunk of Tampa and, from what I understand, would love to own the whole damn town."

Murphy didn't miss the hint of bitterness in George's voice. "And I take it you're not a fan of that plan."

"Don't get me wrong, I'm all about tourism—it's what keeps Tampa on the map—but we are more than that. I just hate to see the locals pushed out of their homes and businesses."

"And yet you work for them," Murphy said hesitantly.

"I don't work for them," George snapped. "I've been telling Mr. Barton for some time he needs to find some new projects. He doesn't agree with FF&C's practices, but he has an obligation to keep his crew working. They have bills, families to feed."

"And so he sleeps with the devil," Murphy mused out loud, stealing Joe's comment about Murphy's new employer.

"We all do things we're not always proud of."

Ain't that the truth. Murphy took a large gulp of his beer and stared down into the amber fluid. "What would happen if FF&C was proven corrupt?"

George laughed without mirth. "That's already a well-known fact, and yet they still conduct business as usual."

Murphy was half-tempted to tell George what he'd heard, but he held back. He needed to tell Joe. Joe would know what to do with the information.

Chapter Eighteen

JOE SLAMMED his phone onto the desk and dropped his head into his hands. He'd been trying to call Murphy for hours, but he wasn't answering. He'd heard the seriousness in Murphy's voice when he'd said, "It's important." Something was wrong. Joe had been worried enough that he'd run upstairs, but after numerous minutes of pounding on the apartment door with no response, he'd given up.

Normally, his cell phone was always in his pocket or close at hand, but he'd forgotten it on his desk and spent most of the day before working on his beach house and doing his best not to think about Murphy. It hadn't gone so well—he always seemed to be thinking about him. The one time Murphy really needed him and Joe had forgotten his goddamn phone. What a dumbass.

His cell phone rang. He checked the display, and his heart skipped a beat when he saw Murphy's name. He flipped the phone open and pressed it to his ear. "Murphy?"

"Yeah, it's me."

The sound of Murphy's voice set Joe's gut fluttering. "Hi. I've been trying to get ahold of you. Forgot my stupid cell in my office last night. Did you get my message?"

"I got it. I really need to talk to you."

Joe tensed. "What's wrong?"

"I don't want to talk about it on the phone. I have a few more errands to run, but can we meet later?"

Dread settled into Joe, and he had to swallow around the lump that formed in his throat. This was it. Murphy was moving on, ending what had only too recently begun to spark between them.

"Yes, of course, but can you give me a hint as to what's up?"

"I can't. I have to go. Do you want me to come to you or—"

"I'm at the café. What time will you be home?"

Joe heard a rustling sound and a brief silence. "I should be at the apartment at three."

Joe didn't miss the way Murphy referred to the place as the apartment rather than home. It didn't bode well. He'd hoped Murphy would want to stay even after the renovations were done. Apparently there was little hope of that.

"I'll be there."

The tension through the phone line was palpable, and Joe wanted to demand Murphy tell him what the hell was going on, but he knew it was in vain.

"Murphy?"

"Hold on a second, I have another call," Murphy said eventually.

A click sounded and nothing but silence came through the line. Joe waited. Each tick of the clock increased the anxiety settling into Joe, until his neck was stiff and his head began to throb.

"Sorry about that," Murphy apologized when he came back on line. "I had another call I had to take."

Joe was curious about who Murphy would be talking to, but once again he knew he dared not ask. "That's okay. I'm not doing anything important at the moment anyway."

"I'm sorry, but I really have to go. I'll see you around three."

"Not even a little hint as to what the topic of discussion is going to be?"

"I would if I could. See you at three."

Before Joe could say another word, the line went dead. He squeezed his eyes shut and tried to remember how to breathe. He'd been fooling himself about Murphy. He'd already wormed his way past Joe's tough outward façade, and now that he was ready to share his feelings with Murphy, it appeared Murphy was going to end it. What else could it be? At least he was man enough to do it in person rather than via text.

It didn't make Joe feel even a shred better.

A knock sounded on the door. Joe sighed. "Come in."

"Hey, Joe. Got a second?" Kallie asked.

"I guess. C'mon in."

Kallie frowned and perched on the corner of Joe's desk. "Everything all right?"

"I'm fine." Joe did his best to smile, but he couldn't quite pull it off.

"You've always been a terrible liar. Anything I can do?"

Joe laid his hand on Kallie's thigh. "Don't pay me any mind. I'm being foolish."

Kallie held his hand. "This about Murphy?"

"Yeah. He finally called me back."

"Is he okay?"

Joe nodded sadly. She knew something was up between him and Murphy. Pretty hard to hide when he'd been moping around and Murphy hadn't been in Kaffeinate the past few days for his morning coffee. She was a smart girl, could easily put two and two together.

"He wants to talk to me about something," Joe answered.

Kallie's frown deepened. "And he didn't say what?"

"No, but I have a pretty good idea what it's about."

"You're assuming you know. You do know what they say about assuming?"

"Yeah, yeah, I've been accused of being worse than an ass before." Joe pushed his chair back and stood. He didn't want to talk about it. His head hurt and his heart felt heavy. "Hey, I was about to order lunch. You want anything?"

"Nice way to change the subject. You haven't even had breakfast yet."

Joe ran his hand through his hair. "I know. I just really don't want to talk about it right now. But I'll be sure to find you if I need a shoulder to cry on."

"That doesn't sound good."

Joe waved a dismissive hand. "Seriously, ignore me. I'm in a funky mood. So what did you need?"

"Whatever it was doesn't seem all that important anymore." Kallie headed for the door. Halfway there, she stopped and spun around. "Oh crap, yeah, the cash register is locked up again."

"Did you try a hammer?" The used and outdated register should have been replaced long ago.

"I would have if I could have found one."

"Let me see if I can locate one for you." Joe was thankful for the distraction.

Kallie preceded him out of the office, laid a hand on his arm, and peered up at him with a stern expression. "I know it's none of my business, but I really hope things work out between you and Murphy. I can tell you two care about each other, but you're both so damn stubborn."

"It will work out the way it's meant to." He leaned down and kissed her cheek. "Now, let's go take out some frustration on that old piece of machinery."

THERE HADN'T been a whole lot of sleep to be found the night before. He'd spent the entire evening fretting about Joe not returning his call, what he'd discovered, and whether he was going to show up at the jobsite in the morning.

All day, he questioned his decision to work at the Calm Winds Resort. He knew he'd made the right choice. He hadn't been able to come up with a believable story as to why he needed the day off and in the end figured if he would have any chance of BMC keeping him on other projects, he'd better do what they were paying him for. He vacillated between unease and irritation all day and nearly jumped up and down with glee when George texted him that it was quitting time.

After pushing through the doors and stepping out into the bright afternoon sunshine, Murphy couldn't get in the van fast enough. He was practically vibrating as he waited for George. *C'mon, c'mon, c'mon.* Murphy was actually considering leaving a note and running back to the office and his car. The only reason he didn't follow through with his plan was because George finally appeared.

George slid into the passenger seat. "I was concerned your ass was on fire, the way you bolted out the door."

"Sorry, I have a date. A bit excited, ya know."

George arched a brow. "She must be something pretty special."

Murphy held his gaze. "He is."

George didn't so much as flinch. "Well, let's get going before we get stuck in afternoon rush hour."

Murphy never knew how someone would react when they discovered he was gay. In his experience, the macho bullshit he came across in the production and construction industries left him believing the vast majority of men in those two lines of work were bigoted assholes. It was refreshing to find George didn't fall into that line of thinking.

As Murphy maneuvered through the streets, he and George engaged in small talk, mainly about his new grandson. Once at the office, Murphy pulled into an empty spot, cut the engine, and sprung from the van.

"Damn, you really are an anxious thing," George drawled.

He was, but probably not for the reasons George was thinking. Murphy tossed the keys to George and pulled his own from his pocket. "Actually, I just need to talk to him, is all," Murphy explained. "See you tomorrow."

He was halfway to his car when George called out. "Hey, Murphy?"

Murphy stopped and turned around. "Yeah?"

"If this talk with Mr. Special doesn't go the way you hope, maybe you could do me a favor."

"Sure, what is it?"

"Get my son out of my basement. I'm tired of hearing him complain about the fact there aren't any nice guys in Tampa."

Murphy laughed. Now he knew why George hadn't batted an eye; he had a gay son. It instantly made Murphy like him all the more, not because he had a gay son but because he obviously accepted his son's sexuality.

"I'll keep that in mind."

MURPHY PACED back and forth, wringing his clammy hands. Christ, he was nervous. He had no idea how Joe would react when he told him what he'd overheard. Murphy had witnessed Joe's fiery temper and could only hope he could talk some sense into him if he was hell-bent on confronting Mr. Fields.

A soft rap on the door had Murphy freezing midstep, and his heart rate sped. It was about time he learned just how much restraint Joe had. Hopefully it was better than that of when they tried to refrain from sex. That thought put a smile on Murphy's face.

He headed to the door and opened it. "Joe. Hi."

Joe stood there, looking more unsure of himself than Murphy had ever seen. There wasn't a single trace of the smug smile, and his normally proud posture was nonexistent.

He seemed to be looking at the doorframe rather than at Murphy. "You said you had something you wanted to talk about."

Murphy touched Joe's elbow. "Look at me, would you?" Joe shifted his gaze to meet Murphy's. "I'm sorry I've been so cryptic. I didn't think it was a good idea to talk over the phone."

"I think I may need a drink." Joe looked away, chewing his lower lip. "Are you going to invite me in?"

Murphy stepped back to allow Joe entry. He shut the door and locked it behind Joe. "Sorry, I've only got beer and water. I can run down to the corner store if you need something stronger."

Joe leaned against the island with a weary expression on his face. "You tell me. You think I need something stronger?"

Murphy took Joe's hand and brought it to his mouth. He kissed his fingertips, then laced their fingers together. "I think whiskey would be counterproductive. What I'm about to tell you may…." Murphy shook his head. "No maybe about it. You're going to be pissed."

For a moment Joe was silent. He was looking at Murphy with an indefinable expression. Then the look was gone before Murphy could figure out what it was. Joe pulled his hand free. "I think I'll have that beer."

Murphy went to the fridge and pulled out two bottles of beer. When he turned around, Joe was slumped on one of the barstools, looking completely lost. Murphy's chest tightened to see Joe looking so distressed, and he wasn't looking forward to making the poor man feel even worse. He set one of the beers down in front of him and took a long pull from the other.

Joe nearly downed his entire beer in one gulp. Joe swiped the back of his hand over his mouth. "Okay, let's hear it."

"Yesterday, I was inspecting the ductwork on the top floor of Calm Winds." Murphy took another drink and picked at the label on his bottle.

"And?" Joe prodded.

"Right above Mr. Fields's office. I sort of… well…."

Joe visibly tensed. "Just tell me."

Murphy shifted and glanced at the door. Joe's legs were longer, but Murphy was quick. He was pretty sure he could catch Joe before he made it to the door. For good measure, Murphy moved around to the other side of the island. He laid his hand on Joe's shoulder and tugged, encouraging him to turn.

When he did, Murphy situated himself between Joe's knees. "You were right. They are corrupt, and I'm sorry I didn't listen to you."

Joe glared at him. "Goddamn, Murphy, tell me what you heard."

"He plans on getting his hands on your block. He told the other guy that if he couldn't find a way around the historical society, he was to burn the buildings to the ground."

"Are you kidding me?" Joe roared.

"C'mon, Joe, you know I wouldn't kid you about something like that."

Joe was seething, his face turning an ugly shade of red and his lip curling up into a sneer. "Over my dead body."

"I don't think they'd have a problem with that. Mr. Fields is a very powerful, very dangerous man."

"Did he threaten my life? I'll kill the son of a bitch."

Joe tried to shove Murphy out of the way, but Murphy grabbed Joe's shoulders, forcing him to remain sitting. "You can't go over there and start threatening the man."

"It's not a threat," Joe snapped.

"You'll never get past the security guard, and even if you do, what? You actually think you could kill him?" Murphy asked, incredulous.

"It's no less than the fucker deserves. How dare he even think about destroying people's lives, taking away their livelihood, their dreams." Joe shoved at Murphy again. "Now get out of the way."

Again, Murphy held fast, but not without great difficulty. Murphy might have had more bulk, but Joe was still strong. "Joe, dammit, listen to me. You can't go over there. The only thing you'll end up doing is getting yourself thrown in jail, and then what? How are you going to protect Kaffeinate and the rest of the shops?"

Joe stopped struggling and met Murphy's gaze with a fierce expression. "I can't sit here and do nothing."

"That's exactly what you're going to do."

Joe's eyes went wide. "Have you lost your mind?"

"Nope. We are going to sit here, have another beer, and *talk* about this." Murphy laid his palm against Joe's cheek. "Got it?"

For long ticks of the clock, Joe stayed rigid, not responding or saying a word. Just when Murphy was beginning to think Joe wouldn't agree, his shoulders slumped as if he was giving in to defeat.

"Do I have a choice?"

"No, you don't." Murphy pecked Joe on the nose before moving away, secure in the knowledge that Joe wouldn't make a break for the door. Joe was pissed, rightfully so, but he was also a logical man.

Murphy grabbed them a couple more beers, then took the seat next to Joe at the island.

"We should go to the cops."

"And tell them what?" Murphy asked.

"That those unscrupulous bastards are going to set the block ablaze."

Murphy shook his head. "We can't. I was eavesdropping, and besides, you know it will be just their word against mine."

Joe scowled. The grip on his bottle was so hard his knuckles were turning white.

They drank their beers in silence. Murphy didn't know what to say, and he knew Joe needed time to process the information. He could practically hear the wheels turning in Joe's head. He was thankful that Joe hadn't turned on him, done the whole "I told you so" shit. It was nothing less than Murphy deserved, but he was still glad he didn't have to hear it or see the disapproval on Joe's face.

"You know, it's funny," Joe finally commented.

"I really don't see anything comical about the situation."

"You're right, but when I first got your message and then your call, you telling me you couldn't tell me on the phone… I actually thought you were coming here to tell me you didn't want to see me anymore."

"To be honest, I've thought of that a time or two."

"Really?"

Murphy nodded.

"And are you still thinking that way?"

Murphy gawked at him. "I just told you some lunatic wants to set your business on fire, and you're worried about whether I want to see you or not?"

"I think the situation would be easier to deal with if I knew you were going to be around." Joe shrugged.

Murphy's chest tightened. For all his posturing, trying to convince himself he didn't need the complications that came with a relationship, he was still here. More importantly, he didn't plan on going anywhere, and as long as Joe wanted him around, that wasn't going to change anytime soon.

He took Joe's hand in his and entwined their fingers. "I'll be here as long as you need me."

Joe's smile was brilliant. "I'm a very needy man."

"I can live with that." He kissed Joe—not an all-consuming, passionate kiss, but one of tenderness and promise. When it ended, Murphy leaned his forehead against Joe's. "Now that that's settled, we need to figure out what we're going to do about Fields."

Chapter Nineteen

JOE DRIFTED back to consciousness with the sound of rain hitting the window and a deafening boom from outside followed by a flash of lightning. Not ready to get up, he pulled at the covers and spent an unmeasured amount of time watching the rain paint abstract images on the bedroom window. He was warm, content, and only needed one more thing to make it perfect. He reached out to pull Murphy close, but the sheets next to him were cool to the touch.

Frowning, Joe pushed himself to a sitting position, rubbed the sleep out of his eyes, and squinted around the room. "Murphy?"

"In here," Murphy called from the master bathroom. "Be out in a second."

Joe heard Murphy shuffling around behind the closed door. The water came on briefly, and then the door swung open and Murphy sauntered out, a towel wrapped around his hips, rivulets of water running down his muscular chest.

"Sorry, didn't mean to wake you. I needed a shower."

"It was the thunder, but I wish you would have. I would have been more than willing to wash your back for you."

"Lucky for me I take plenty of showers. Can I get a rain check?"

"Absolutely." Joe snagged Murphy's wrist the second he got close enough and pulled him to the bed. "Mmmm. Warm, damp, and you smell good too."

Laughing, Murphy pecked Joe on the nose. "At least one of us does. You smell like sex and morning breath."

"Your fault. Another reason you should have woke me. I would have been minty-fresh and -smelling too. Then maybe I could have talked you into a little morning delight."

Murphy nuzzled the side of Joe's neck. "No time like the present, but I'd suggest you hurry up as I might have to start without you."

Joe palmed Murphy's cock, squeezing hard. "Don't you dare, or I may take an extra-long, extra-thorough cleaning. And you know how good lathering up my dick feels."

Heat flared in Murphy's eyes, and he slapped Joe's hand away from his crotch. "You've got five minutes."

Not wasting a second, Joe leaped from the bed and rushed to the bathroom. While standing under the warm spray, the conversation from the night before came rushing back. He obviously had it way worse for Murphy than he'd thought. There was a very rich, very corrupt bastard out there who wanted to destroy eight years of blood, sweat, and tears with a single match. Instead of that pressing matter being the first thing on his mind when he woke, it was Murphy and getting his rocks off. Again.

The problem with dealing in reality at the moment was there was really nothing he could do about it. Every instinct in Joe was screaming to race down to Mr. Fields's office and confront the bastard. The logical side of him knew Murphy was right. Nothing good could come of going off half-cocked with rage and ending up in jail. They had no proof, and the way in which Murphy had obtained the info couldn't be used legally. If they tipped Mr. Fields off, he'd no doubt use his wealth and power to get out of it. Then where would Joe be? At least he knew what Fields's plan was and might actually be able to prevent it. If the bastard changed the plan because he found out Murphy had been eavesdropping, then there was no telling what his next attempt would consist of. Worse still, it could put Murphy at risk. Completely unacceptable.

With their focus on their dicks, it wasn't likely they would come up with a solution to the Fields problem. Nope, better to ease that itch first, and then they could try to figure out how to keep the block safe.

His plan set, Joe shoved down his worry. He had a very sexy, very naked man in his bed waiting for him. He turned off the taps and dried off quickly. His arousal renewed, he hurried to brush his teeth and get back to Murphy.

"Joe?" Murphy called out.

"Mmm hmm," Joe responded around a mouthful of toothpaste.

"You have thirty seconds, or I'm starting without you."

Joe looked up and met his wide-eyed reflection. *Oh hell no, you don't.* Spit, rinse, and he was out the door, not bothering to turn off the light or grab a towel for his still-dripping wet hair.

Murphy gave Joe a mischievous smile. "Ten seconds."

Joe took a flying leap onto the bed, making the springs squeak, and Murphy let out a loud *oomph* when Joe grabbed him and rolled them. Before Murphy could protest, Joe took Murphy's mouth in a deep, toe-curling kiss.

One of Murphy's legs wound around Joe's hips. Groin to groin, they rocked together. Murphy's erection rubbing against his caused Joe's to tingle and his breath to speed up. The heat and delicious friction was so damn perfect, he rutted harder, faster, wanting more of the pleasure-filled sensation. Joe didn't want it to end. He could come just from the sensual kisses and Murphy's dick sliding against his. Murphy, however, had other plans.

"I need to be inside you. Get the lube."

As good as Murphy's body felt against his, he knew it could be even better. He loved the way Murphy filled him, stretched him. A deep rumbling groan worked its way out of his chest. Still, he was unable to lose the heat of Murphy's body. He tightened his arm around Murphy's waist and rolled them until Murphy was on top of him. He took Murphy's mouth in a slow, lazy kiss while he groped around in the bedside table until he finally found the lube.

Murphy didn't seem to mind the position change. He returned the kiss with aggressive passion, dominating it. He rocked while exploring every inch of Joe's mouth until they were both breathless.

Murphy ended the kiss and smiled. "Are you trying to distract me?"

"Why would I do that? I'm simply enjoying each and every second."

Murphy's smile grew even wider. "So am I. Now, about that lube."

Joe held the tube up. "Ta-da."

Without moving his gaze from Joe's, Murphy took the tube from him, then sat back on his calves. He poured a small amount of lube onto his fingers, rubbing it in with his thumb.

The lust-filled look in Murphy's eyes and the way he was taking his dear sweet time slicking up his fingers made the anticipation within Joe build until he was practically vibrating with need.

Murphy made him wait a few seconds longer. Just when Joe thought he would burst, Murphy nudged Joe's thigh with his clean hand. "Spread for me. Show me that sweet hole."

Joe placed his feet on the mattress, spread his legs, and lifted his ass. He was rewarded with two slick fingers teasing his hole, tapping,

tapping, then pushing ever so slowly into him. Joe gasped and bore down, taking Murphy's fingers deeper inside him.

Murphy scissored his fingers, and the burn made Joe gasp, but it quickly turned into a long, drawn-out moan as ecstasy pulsed through his body. A slight turn of Murphy's wrist and he nailed Joe's sweet spot. Joe cried out, back arching.

"Damn, you're hot," Murphy murmured. "Love watching you like this."

Joe tried to reply, say something, but he couldn't form the words, the pleasure overwhelming him. His body twitched, cock bobbing and leaking on Joe's stomach. He was so close, a few hard pulls and he'd be coming. He reached for his erection.

Murphy pulled his fingers free and blocked Joe from taking himself in hand. "Oh, no, you don't. I've got plans for that."

"So did I," Joe groaned. He wanted to, wanted badly to come, but instead, he grabbed the headboard to keep from giving in to the temptation. He raised his hips, thrusting a couple of times. "C'mon, Murphy. Touch me."

Murphy patted Joe's thigh before snatching the condom up from the table and opening it.

"That's cold, man. You know what I mean."

"I promise to make it up to you." Murphy didn't tease any further. He rolled the condom down his length, then guided the head of his cock to Joe's hole.

They locked gazes, Joe scarcely breathing when Murphy languidly entered him in one long stroke, until he was balls-deep within Joe.

"Love the way your ass feels around me," Murphy groaned. He bit down on his lip and thrust gently, once, twice, a third time before pulling all the way out and pushing in again hard and fast.

Joe slid his arms beneath his knees, pulling his legs to his chest, and lifted his ass, forcing Murphy even deeper with each hard thrust. Murphy shifted slightly and Joe cried out when Murphy pegged his prostate.

"Damn! That's it, right there," Joe said.

Murphy did it again, over and over again, until Joe was begging and moaning, rocking into each thrust and pleading with his body until he was on the verge of orgasm, the intensity so great he could barely contain it. He closed his eyes and gritted his teeth, trying to stave off the inevitable for a few more minutes.

Murphy's strokes became irregular, and when Joe opened his eyes, Murphy's head was tipped back slightly, lips parted as he chased his release. The sight before Joe stole his breath and nearly pushed him over the edge.

When Murphy gave one more hard thrust, then froze, Joe knew he no longer had to hold back, and seconds later he was proven right when Murphy cried out Joe's name. Joe released the tight hold he had on his orgasm and tumbled over the edge.

How long Joe was held in that blissful, perfect state, he wasn't sure. The only thing he knew was pure pleasure—he soared with it, and when he floated back down, Murphy was right there.

Joe released the hold he had on his legs and wrapped his arms tightly around Murphy. "Damn, I needed that."

Murphy grunted in response.

Joe rested his chin on Murphy's head, drawing patterns with his fingertips up and down Murphy's spine. Joe wished they could lie here forever, boneless and satisfied. Just the two of them shielded from the problems outside of their warm cocoon. But that was wishful thinking. They were only getting a short reprieve from the harsh reality.

"We need to decide what we're going to do about FF&C," Murphy said softly, as if he'd been reading Joe's mind.

Joe grimaced. "I know, but I'm not ready to ruin my postorgasmic buzz just yet, are you?"

"Nope." Murphy rolled slightly and pushed himself up closer to Joe's side.

Joe held Murphy, and within moments Murphy was fast asleep, making those cute little noises Joe loved. Joe pulled him in tighter, letting Murphy's warmth lull him to sleep.

Chapter Twenty

ONE WOULD have thought it was Murphy's livelihood that had been threatened, by the way his heart was hammering and his stomach was flip-flopping. Crazy that he seemed to be the one freaking out while Joe sat across the table from him, looking like he didn't have a care in the world.

Murphy had seen Joe's fiery temper, been on the receiving end of it, and yet here Joe sat, less than twenty-four hours after finding out about what Mr. Fields had said, appearing calm and collected, eating pancakes.

"How can you eat that?"

Joe looked up with a confused expression. "What? You don't like them? Would you prefer something else?"

"No, they taste fine, but now that I don't want to jump your bones, I can't help but think about what I overheard, and it's messing with my appetite. I'm surprised it's not messing with yours."

"You don't want to jump my bones?" Joe asked, sounding and looking wounded.

Murphy gawked at him. "Seriously? That's what you took out of that statement?"

Joe grinned around his mug before taking a sip. "I always want to jump your bones."

Murphy threw his hands up. "I give up. You're a very strange man, Joe Sterling."

Joe popped a large bite of pancake into his mouth, speaking around it while he chewed. "Trust me, I know how bad the situation is. I woke up last night and lay there a long time thinking about it." Joe washed his food down with a swig of coffee. "I tell you, my first inclination is to storm down there and beat that son of a bitch to a bloody pulp. However, I kept thinking about what you said, and you're right. Not much I can do to protect my block from behind bars."

Some of the tension eased from Murphy. He hadn't realized until that moment that the idea of Joe going off and doing something crazy was what had Murphy all in knots. The nauseated feeling also let loose and he was able to eat his breakfast.

He munched on a piece of bacon while asking, "Tell me, if you don't plan on going to jail, what are you going to do?"

"I haven't gotten it all worked out, but I will."

"I'm sure you will," Murphy assured him. "I can't tell you how sorry I was for not listening to you. I've already told George I will not work for that bastard. He's trying to get me transferred to another jobsite." Murphy lowered his eyes, not able to hold Joe's gaze. "I'm not proud of the fact that I did yesterday, but only because George asked me to. I told him I'd quit if he couldn't get me a transfer."

"It's okay. Honestly, I understand."

Joe went silent while he finished his breakfast. He cleared the table and did the dishes without saying a word, a thoughtful expression on his face, as if he was thinking about what Murphy had said. Murphy didn't push, but it was strange. Joe liked to talk, did it all the time. Hell, Murphy wouldn't be surprised if Joe did it in his sleep. Although, as hard of a sleeper as Murphy was, he might never know for sure.

Joe was back in his chair with a fresh cup of coffee before the silence got to Murphy.

"Okay, I'm going nuts. What are you thinking about?"

"I'm not sure if I should tell you. I'm still weighing the pros and cons," Joe explained.

"What the hell is that supposed to mean?"

Joe let out a heavy sigh. "I have this thought that keeps popping into my head, but I'm worried about how you'll take it."

"Only one way to find out."

Joe studied him for a moment. Murphy could see the conflict etched in the lines in Joe's face. Then Joe shook his head. "No, I can't ask you. It's a bad idea. I can't put you in danger."

"Dammit, Joe. Would you just tell me and let me decide for myself?" It came out sounding much more snappish than he meant it to, but the cryptic shit was getting on his nerves.

"I was thinking if you were to go back into those ducts, but this time take a listening device, we could get proof."

Murphy's eyes went wide.

"I told you it was a bad idea." Joe pushed to his feet, taking his coffee cup with him. He started pacing.

It took a few ticks of the clock before Murphy was able to process what Joe proposed. It wasn't a bad idea per se, but…. He thrummed his fingers on the table while considering it. "I could pull it off," Murphy assured him. "Problem is, it's illegal to record someone without a warrant."

Joe froze midstep and glared at Murphy. Fire ignited in his eyes. "Illegal? The guy wants to set an entire city block on fire, and you're talking to me about a recorder being illegal?"

There was the passion Murphy was used to seeing in Joe. It was odd that when Joe got fired up, it both turned Murphy on and pissed him off. "Because two wrongs make a right?"

"Are you stupid? I can't believe you are even going to compare the two!"

Irritation won out. Murphy jumped up and stalked over to Joe and stabbed his finger in Joe's chest. "You call me that one more time and I swear I'll kick your ass."

They stood toe to toe, both posturing. Joe tried to use his height, staring down at Murphy in an obvious attempt to intimidate him. *Well, fuck that.* He wasn't even a little bit cowed.

He poked Joe in the chest again. "I mean it."

Joe continued to glare at him for a moment longer, but apparently good sense and logic kicked in. Joe's shoulders slumped. "Damn, I did it again. When I get pissed, shit just comes out of my mouth I don't mean." Joe slid an arm around Murphy's waist and tugged. "Forgive me?"

Murphy remained rigid, holding on to his irritation. Joe wasn't the first person Murphy had met who'd said something hateful when angry. Hell, he might have done it a time or two hundred in his lifetime. He'd always been a bit snippy and quick to react without thinking. Dylan certainly had been on the receiving end of Murphy's temper. He suspected Dylan provoked him on purpose. Dylan did like his drama.

"Well?" Joe asked, pulling Murphy from his musings.

"Yeah, I forgive you, but watch that forked tongue of yours. I'm on your side here, remember? I'm only trying to help."

"I know." Joe kissed Murphy's forehead. "Sorry for being an utter and complete dick."

"Maybe not a complete one…."

Murphy tried to hold back the grin that threatened but was unsuccessful when Joe added, "Just an utter one."

They both laughed, and the tension in the room disappeared.

"How about we take our coffee to the couch, kick back, and see if we can come up with a plan?" Joe suggested.

"I'm all for it, except the couch part."

"Why is that?"

Murphy freed himself from Joe's embrace. He grabbed his mug from the table and took it to the counter to refill it. "You still want to jump my bones, so I figure the only way you're going to stay focused on the task at hand is to keep a table between us." He held up the carafe. "Refill?"

"Good point." Joe snorted. He held up his mug for Murphy to top off.

Through a second pot of coffee, they tossed ideas back and forth, trying to come up with a way to out Fields's corruption that didn't include either of them going to jail or exposing them to unnecessary dangers. They agreed planting the listening device and monitoring Fields's office was a good idea. The problem was what to do with the incriminating evidence once they obtained it.

Joe wanted to take it straight to Fields and essentially blackmail the bastard into backing off. Maybe Murphy had watched one too many crime shows, because the only thing he could see coming out of that plan was Joe's bits washing up on the beach. They had to figure out something that wouldn't reveal their involvement.

"How about we send it to the local police chief anonymously?" Joe suggested.

"I'm sure they'd somehow be able to trace it back to us. Plus, that's only if they took it seriously, or God forbid someone who is in Fields's back pocket heard it." A light popped on in Murphy's head. "That's it!"

"What?"

"We'll send it anonymously."

"But you just said—"

Murphy held up a single finger. "We're not going to send it to the authorities. We're going to send it to the *Tampa Bay Times*."

Joe stared at him, blank. Seconds later Joe's light joined Murphy's because his face lit up. "I know exactly who to send it to! A couple years ago, Mitch Leverette did a piece for the *Tampa Tribune* on the environmental laws FF&C was violating. Soon after the story came out, he and the editor in chief resigned and the story was quashed. Mitch is now with the *Times*."

"Perfect. Now all we have to do is get the proof."

"It's settled." Joe went to his feet and held out a hand for Murphy. "Let's go."

Murphy took the hand without hesitation but asked, "Where are we going?"

"To celebrate having a plan." Joe pulled Murphy toward the bedroom.

"Seriously, Joe?"

"Hey, I'm the one who always wants to jump your bones, remember? Plus, it's the one thing we never argue or fight about."

The instant they were in the room, Murphy yanked his hand free, then shoved Joe toward the bed. "Damn fine point."

"I have my moments," Joe said smugly.

"And I have mine," Murphy responded just before he jumped Joe's bones.

Chapter Twenty-One

SETTING THE listening device had been easy. Damn good thing, too, since George had gotten Murphy transferred to another jobsite two days later. It sucked that it was an hour's drive south of Tampa, but it was worth it to have FF&C's name taken off his paycheck. He hadn't told George about what he'd overheard—he didn't need to. What he hadn't figured out was why BMC was still taking jobs from the corrupt bastards. George hadn't told Murphy why, but he could tell it was a sore spot with him. Murphy had a suspicion that George wouldn't be disappointed if FF&C went down. However, so far it wasn't looking too good. Nearly two weeks and Fields hadn't said one thing incriminating.

Maybe today would be their lucky day. He pulled open the door on Kaffeinate and stepped inside.

"Good morning, Murphy," Kallie greeted.

"Morning, sunshine." Murphy glanced around the café. There was one person sitting near the window, but other than that, the place was empty. The only good thing about having to get up an hour earlier with his new job was no line for coffee.

Kallie pointed to the counter, and a smile spread across Murphy's face. Sitting at the first stool was a large iced coffee, sweet roll, and the newspaper, open to the sports section.

He took a seat and grabbed his coffee taking a large drink. "Wow, I'm predictable. Thanks, Kallie."

"Don't thank me, thank him."

Murphy looked to where Kallie was pointing, and his smile grew impossibly larger when he spotted Joe stepping through the door. He sauntered over to stand in front of Murphy. "Morning."

It was only one innocent word, but damn, Murphy's blood instantly heated. Whether it was the smug expression on Joe's face, the seductive tone of his voice, or simply that Murphy was a horndog didn't matter. The outcome was the same—instant boner.

"Stop that."

"I didn't do anything." Joe leaned in, his lips brushing the shell of Murphy's ear. "Yet."

Murphy clamped down on the shudder that threatened. This morning had been the first time in a week that Murphy hadn't woken up next to Joe. They had fallen into an exhausting routine: morning sex, coffee, work, sex, dinner, sex. Murphy had put his foot down and stayed in the apartment over the coffee shop the night before. When Joe protested, Murphy had argued that his dick would fall off if he stayed one more night. Joe had grudgingly given in, if for no other reason than to spare Murphy the pain of becoming a eunuch.

"Yeah, and you're not going to anytime soon." Murphy assured him. He wasn't about to give in to Joe's desires until he could touch his dick without wincing. Stupid thing wasn't cooperating, though: it was hard and ready to go. He sighed.

"Aww, but I miss you." Joe pushed out his lips in an attempt to pout. It didn't work.

"It hasn't even been twenty-four hours," Murphy reminded him. He patted Joe's arm. "I'm pretty sure you will survive one more day without sex."

Joe's eyes went comically wide. "You mean I don't get any tonight either? What have I done for you to treat me so badly?"

Murphy refrained from rolling his eyes. "You hurt my wanker, so if anyone is being punished, it's me." He smiled, then shoved a big bite of sweet roll into his mouth.

Joe sighed dramatically. Murphy knew he was doing it for effect. Bastard looked way too satisfied with himself. If Murphy could have done it without causing permanent damage to himself, he might consider it.

"So, are blow jobs out of the question?"

Murphy gave Joe an exasperated look, not even bothering to respond, and instead took another big bite of his roll.

"Okay, okay," Joe conceded with an exaggerated sigh. "No sex, no blow jobs, not even a single caress to your dick if you'll come stay with me tonight. I promise nothing but cuddles will happen in my bed."

"I don't cuddle," Murphy insisted.

Joe held up his hands. "I meant me. I will cuddle you. All you have to do is sleep next to me."

Murphy considered it for a moment. "All right, but you're keeping your drawers on. I don't want to be waking up with you knocking at my back door." He pointed a finger at Joe. "Got it?"

Joe beamed. "Got it." He leaned in and gave Murphy a sweet kiss. "I have paperwork to do. See you after work."

"I'll be there." Murphy grabbed Joe's hair and kissed him soundly. No sense in Murphy being the only one going to work with a hard, unsatisfied dick.

Chapter Twenty-Two

IF HE were a meaner man, Joe would be crowing, "Told you so." Murphy should have known they wouldn't be able to keep their hands off each other. Silly, silly man for even thinking it. Lying spent and panting across his bed, who was he to complain about Murphy's lack of restraint. Joe probably should feel bad that Murphy would have a hard time wearing shorts, but he simply couldn't find it in himself to care. He felt too good.

Murphy rolled and propped his head up on his hand. "You know what?"

"What?" Joe kissed Murphy's nose.

Murphy narrowed his eyes and huffed out a breath. "You're going to pay for this."

Laughing, Joe rolled, mirroring Murphy's position. "I'm not even sorry a little bit."

Murphy's scowl faded into a sly grin. "I didn't figure you would be, but…. Who am I kidding. That was amazing, sore dick and all."

"The best." Joe slid his free hand down to grasp Murphy's hip. "Want to do it again?"

"Oh hell to the no, you can't possibly—" Obviously, he figured out Joe was teasing on his own. "Fucker!"

"That would be you. I'm the fuckee." Joe chuckled.

Laughing, Murphy shoved Joe onto his back and rested his head on Joe's chest. "We better substitute my sweet roll breakfast with Wheaties."

"Done."

They lay there together, enjoying the quiet and the warmth. But, eventually the drying come on Joe's belly began to itch. "I better get cleaned up before we get stuck together forever."

"Would make working and eating a little difficult," Murphy responded sleepily.

Joe extricated himself from Murphy and did a quick cleanup in the bathroom. He brought a warm rag back and handed it to Murphy before sliding into bed next to him. Joe decided on a ten-minute nap before he made dinner.

Murphy had a different idea.

"We've been seeing each other for quite some time, but I don't feel as if I know you all that well. Tell me something I don't know."

"Hmm, let me think." Joe took the rag from Murphy and tossed it on the floor. He pulled him into an embrace, encouraging Murphy to lay his head on Joe's chest. "I like having sex with you."

Murphy swatted him playfully. "I said something I didn't know, you dork."

"Oh yeah, right. I was valedictorian of my high school class."

"That's cool. Doesn't surprise me, but very cool. I sucked in high school. If it hadn't been for football, I probably would have failed."

"I seriously doubt that. Did you say you went through trade school?"

Murphy drew random patterns on Joe's chest with his fingertip. "Only because they didn't make me take any English classes."

"Doubt that. You have a great vocabulary."

"Yup, I can use twenty-five different terms for 'fuck you.'" Murphy chuckled.

"See," Joe agreed. "Okay, your turn. Tell me something I don't know about you."

Murphy was silent for a moment while he continued to draw patterns. He then lifted his head and looked at Joe with a cheeky grin. "I performed in a drag show when I was eighteen."

Joe burst out laughing. "You are not serious."

"Yup. Six-inch stilettos and all. I was hot."

Joe cackled so hard he choked on it.

"Serves you right, laughing at me."

"Sorry, babe," Joe got out around a snort. He ran his hand over Murphy's jaw. "I'm just having a really hard time picturing you in a dress."

"Okay, so I wasn't a very convincing queen." Murphy snickered. "All right, it's your turn again."

"I'd love to go to Europe, but I'm afraid of planes and boats."

"Boats? Dude, you live on the ocean."

"And? I had a bad experience with my tugboat while in the tub."

"Whatever."

"I'm serious. Let me guess, you're not afraid of anything."

"Nope. Just call me Barney Badass."

"Or Eugene."

Murphy grabbed Joe's nipple and pinched it hard until Joe yelped. "Uncle! I mean ouch! Barney, let go!"

"That's better," Murphy said with a satisfied grin. He rubbed the abused nub. "Actually, there is one thing I'm afraid of."

"Do tell."

"Wo...."

Murphy's voice was so low and he seemed to be mumbling, so Joe couldn't make out what he was saying. "What was that?"

"Worms."

"Wh—"

Murphy pinched Joe's lips closed. "Shut it. Not all worms, just those big nasty night crawlers." Murphy shuddered.

Joe slapped Murphy's hand away. "Snakes I get, spiders, even skunks, but worms?"

"Our pool burst when I was like five, and all these worms came up out of the soaked ground all wriggling, crawling across my feet, slimy, and just... eww."

"Okay, I can see how that could traumatize a kid. How about we get up and you can tell me more about your past while I cook us dinner?"

Murphy stretched up and pressed his lips to Joe's. "Second best offer I've had all night."

Chapter Twenty-Three

MURPHY REACHED out to knock on Joe's door, but it flew open before his knuckles made contact.

"Get in here," Joe said excitedly. He grabbed Murphy's hand and pulled him into the apartment. "You've got to hear this."

"No way."

Joe shut the door behind them, then placed a big sloppy kiss on Murphy's cheek. "We got the son of a bitch!"

Murphy tingled with excitement as Joe fired up his laptop. Thirteen days they'd been waiting for something, anything that they could use against Fields, and it looked as if their wait was finally over.

"What did he say?"

"Hold on, you can hear it for yourself." Joe typed at the keyboard, pulled up a program, then turned up the speakers. He rested his hand on the mouse. "Sit back and enjoy the show."

Murphy sat on the couch next to Joe and listened.

"I've tried everything, sir. There is no way around the historical classification."

"I recognize that voice. It's the bookkeeping-looking dude," Murphy exclaimed.

"That's John Clare, the governor's assistant." He turned up the volume. "Listen."

"Then try harder. I'm not paying you to try. I want results!" Fields's voice was followed by a loud bang as if he'd slammed his hand down on his desk.

"Mr. Fields, please," squeaked Clare. "I assure you, I have tried everything. Money, threats, soul damnation—the council refuses to budge on their position."

"Did Chandler deny you? Did you tell him I'd release the files if I didn't get what I want?" Fields asked.

Joe nudged Murphy and whispered, "Head of the Tampa building industry service board."

Murphy nodded in acknowledgment.

"I did, sir. He said to tell you he would if he could, but he simply can't do what you ask. He also said he'd put a bullet in his head before he went to prison. He looked like he's about to keel over. He was so white and shaking like a leaf in a windstorm. I honestly believe he'd do it if he could."

"Sick bastard would be better off dead, in my humble opinion," Fields declared. There was the sound of papers rustling, a chair squeaking. "Then I suppose there is no other choice."

Murphy glanced at Joe, whose face had gone red. He was visibly shaking. Whatever was coming next wasn't good.

"People could die," Clare mumbled.

"Would serve them right," Fields snapped. "Can you not appreciate how much money I have lost playing this game? Well, I assure you, I won't lose another red cent!"

"I won't have any part of this. I won't be party to murder."

"Ah, but my dear Mr. Clare, you are already part of it," Fields informed him. His tone of voice was sharp, deadly. "Now you will do exactly as I tell you, or you'll be on the steel slab next to anyone else who gets in my way. Do I make myself perfectly clear?"

Joe scowled, slammed the lid down on his laptop, and jumped to his feet. "I need a drink." He stormed off to the kitchen.

"Is that it?" Murphy asked.

"What the hell do you mean, 'is that it'? Don't you think that's enough?"

Murphy got to his feet and followed Joe, grabbed him by the arm and spun him around. "I'm not the enemy here. I was simply asking if he gave times, dates—you know, so we can be prepared?"

Joe's shoulders slumped and he clung to Murphy. "I know that. Jesus, Murphy, I'm sorry. I just don't know what to do with this anger. I feel like it's engulfing me, drowning me. I need an outlet."

Murphy held him. Joe was shaking so hard, Murphy worried the man would explode if he let go. It was one thing to hear it secondhand, but it was a whole other level to hear a man planning the destruction of your dream. Your murder. Murphy was pissed beyond all reason. He could only imagine how much more powerful it was in Joe.

"How about we get that drink and figure out what we want to write in our letter to Mr. Leverette. Hmm?"

Joe nodded. "Yeah, okay."

Murphy settled Joe onto a stool at the counter, then poured them each a healthy amount of bourbon. He brought the glasses back to the table and set one down in front of Joe, then took the seat next to him.

"I was giving it some thought. I don't know that we'll need to write a letter along with that recording. It's pretty self-explanatory."

Joe threw back half his drink. "I thought so too. I'd prefer no one discover it was you who set that recorder."

"Nor your involvement."

Joe waved a dismissive hand. "I don't care if they know about me. This isn't your fight, and I'll be damned if I'll allow you to pay the price for me." He threw back the rest of his drink and slammed the glass on the table. Joe's anger was still visibly simmering just below the surface.

Murphy's flared to life. "How dare you say that to me."

Joe blinked. "What?"

"That you don't care if they know about your involvement. These are very dangerous men, Joe. Do you have any clue what it would do to me if, because of the information I obtained, something happened to you? Do you have a clue what kind of guilt I'd have to live with?" Murphy yelled, his voice rising.

JOE LOOKED up at Murphy's outburst, stunned by the venom in his tone and the anger shining in his eyes. "Why are you yelling at me?" Joe snapped. "Can't a guy protect the man he loves?"

Shit! He hadn't meant to say that out loud.

It had been buzzing through Joe's brain lately, but he hadn't planned on examining those feelings too deeply until after this mess with FF&C was cleared up. To say he was an emotional wreck lately was a hell of an understatement.

Joe scooted his chair next to Murphy's and wound an arm around Murphy's shoulders. "I'm sorry. Not really the best time to be making that revelation, is it?"

Murphy's eyes went wide, the shock evident in his eyes and tight features. After a few heartbeats, he leaned forward to lay his head on Joe's shoulder. "Wow. Nothing like throwing a man a curveball. Can we deal with one issue at a time?"

Joe's heart fell. It was a stupid time to be professing his love, he knew that. It still stung like hell that Murphy didn't want to even acknowledge Joe's feelings. "I know. I wish I could take it back." Joe tilted Murphy's chin up to kiss his lips. "Just ignore me. I'm a crazy man right now. Emotions are all whacked out, ya know?"

"Understandable," Murphy said, sounding sincere. "I think we both have had a lot to deal with lately. We'll get through this. Just one thing at a time, okay?"

"Together?"

Murphy ran his hand along Joe's jaw and kissed him gently. "Of course together, silly man."

Joe was relieved that Murphy wasn't dismissing his feelings, only setting the conversation aside for the moment. He could live with that, and the next time they talked about the L word, it certainly wouldn't be while tempers were flying.

"Okay, so we're in agreement we won't send any kind of letter with the recording."

Murphy smiled genuinely. "Whatever you decide, I'm behind you one hundred percent." He patted Joe's face softly. "As long as we don't end up in jail."

"Awesome. Then we are back on the same page," Joe answered. He slid a hand around the back of Murphy's head and pulled him in for a deep kiss. Everything was right in his world for a few glorious moments.

Murphy sat back in his chair, taking his drink with him, and took a sip. "So, when do you want to do this?"

"No time like the present," Joe responded, thankful the awkward moment had passed.

"How are you going to get it to the guy? You can't send it by email; they will be able to track you through your ISP."

"Shit, I hadn't thought about that. Okay…." Joe tapped his fingers against the side of his glass while he stared into it. "What about we drop it off at the paper?"

"Nope, there's a chance they have video or you could be recognized."

"Another good point. Lucky you're mine." The second the words were out, Joe cringed. *Dammit, when will you learn to keep your big mouth shut?*

To Joe's surprise, Murphy leaned forward and laid his free hand on Joe's knee. "Damn right you're lucky to have me. I only wish I could be there to see the look on Fields's face when this story hits the newsstands."

"That would be a sight to behold, for sure." Joe held up his empty glass. "Ready for another?"

"Sure."

Joe poured them each another bourbon, then returned to the island. A horrifying thought occurred to him. "Speaking of video, do you think there is anyway Fields will have video of you setting the device?"

"The building has a shitload of cameras. Definitely a secure building. I had to go through a hell of a background check before I could work there. But I highly doubt they would have them in the ductwork." Murphy stroked the inside seam of Joe's shorts. "I'm sorry I was such a jackass before, when you tried to tell me they were crooked. I want to do what I can to stop them."

Joe had to laugh at the irony of it.

"What?" Murphy demanded. "What's so funny?"

Joe shook his head. "Nothing. Just thinking next time I ought to be more careful what I pray for."

Comprehension lit Murphy's eyes. "You actually prayed for this shit?"

"No, silly man. I certainly didn't pray for arson and murder…. Come to think of it, I did." Joe laughed. "I prayed they would show themselves for the scumballs they were."

"Yeah, you better be careful with that powerful prayer of yours. It could come back and bite you in the ass."

"Actually, I'm not completely opposed to a little ass biting."

Murphy shook his head. "There's that one-track mind I've come to expect."

"This is not completely my fault. I normally have much better control, but you do this to me." Joe pulled Murphy's hand from his thigh to his crotch, letting him feel Joe's growing erection.

Murphy yanked his hand away. "Oh hell no, you don't."

"Aww, c'mon, babe."

"No, and you are not going to persuade me, you damn nympho." Murphy pointed toward the living room. "Now, go get your computer and let's get that on a USB."

Joe pushed out his bottom lip, but the stern look in Murphy's eyes let him know he wasn't going to talk him into sex anytime soon. Poor guy had a sore wiener. Joe doubted he could handle it. Could *he*? Hell yeah. He had it that bad for Murphy and doubted he'd ever get enough.

Chapter Twenty-Four

JOE STEPPED out of his office and bumped into someone. He reached out and grabbed the doorframe to keep from falling on his ass.

"Whoa," Kallie called out. "Watch it."

Joe righted himself, and only then did he notice the pink in Kallie's cheeks and Jeremy on the other side of the door, looking quite guilty. "Well, well, well."

Kallie rolled her eyes. "No well, well, well. I thought you were coming in late."

"Obviously." Joe nudged Jeremy with his elbow. "You dog, you."

Kallie slapped Joe's arm, hard.

"Ow! What the hell was that for?"

"Jeremy simply came in to help me put away supplies."

Joe looked back and forth between Kallie and Jeremy. Both looked like they'd just been caught with their hands in the cookie jar. As often as Kallie had dipped her nose into Joe's love life, he couldn't resist repaying the favor a wee bit.

"Umm, Kallie, we didn't have a delivery."

Kallie put her hands on her hips and glared up at Joe. "Fine, he's here to help me reorganize the stock."

"Uh-huh?"

"C'mon, Jeremy, we have work to do." She grabbed Jeremy's hand and pulled him into the café, Joe right on their heels.

"Jeremy and Kallie, sitting in a tree. K—"

Kallie swirled around and her mouth fell open. "You are so juvenile."

"I know. It's part of my charm."

"Maybe I should check the back room," Jeremy offered.

Kallie flipped on the coffeemakers. "No, you can get those coffee filters filled. Don't let Joe scare you. He's just being an ass."

Joe leaned in close and in a stage whisper said, "Karma is a bitch, isn't it?"

"What the heck is that supposed to mean?"

Joe picked up a napkin dispenser, checking its contents. "How many times have you nosed around my love life?"

"I only involve myself in yours because you need serious help," Kallie pointed out. "I, on the other hand, need no help for my nonexistent love life."

Joe didn't miss the way Jeremy's face fell after Kallie's statement. Poor guy was getting the wrong end of the stick from Joe's teasing. Besides, he was glad to see the two of them together. He'd get the whole story from Kallie later. All he had to do was buy her a couple of fruity alcoholic drinks, and he'd probably learn more than he wanted to. Smiling, he filled the dispenser and went to check the rest of them.

A soft rap on the door had Joe looking up. Alaina, the newspaper carrier, stood outside, waving.

"I got it," Joe called out to Kallie.

Joe went to the front door and unlocked it. "Morning, Alaina. How are you this fine Monday morning?"

Alaina handed him the stack of newspapers with a heavy sigh. "It's *Monday*, Joe."

"First day of the week, darling. Monday is the perfect chance to correct last week's mistakes."

"Yeah, well, if each day is such a gift, I'd like to know where I can return Monday."

"Ohhh, good one." Joe winked.

"See you tomorrow for Tuesday tips."

Joe chuckled. "Yep." He waved goodbye and locked the door behind her.

Six months since Alaina had started delivering the news and they hadn't run out of quotes yet. He briefly wondered if she did the same thing he did: he had an app on his phone that sent him a quote of the day. He wasn't about to tell her. His competitive side wouldn't allow it.

Joe dropped the papers on the counter, and his jaw hit the floor when he read the headline.

A COOL breeze caused Murphy to shiver, and he instinctively reached out for Joe. Murphy frowned when he found only cool sheets on the other side of the bed. He shivered again and grabbed the covers that had pooled around his feet, pulling them up beneath his chin.

The last two weeks, he and Joe had spent nearly every night together, and it surprised Murphy how quickly he'd gotten accustomed to Joe being in his bed. For all his refusal to enter another relationship, Murphy wanted Joe around all the time and missed the man when he wasn't. It went way beyond a physical attraction. Yes, the sex was good, out-of-this-world good, but it was more. So much more.

Murphy rolled to his side and stared out the open window. The colorful lights of the city beyond danced across the walls of the darkened room. His love for Tampa had grown leaps and bounds since he'd moved here. The vibe, the people, and the amazing views were addictive. He was even beginning to get used to the heat. The humidity, not so much. But at least it was becoming bearable. Most of the time. However, the need for air-conditioning among the residents assured he'd always have a job that didn't include smelling like a pickle.

Then there was Joe.

Murphy talked a lot of big talk about keeping Joe at arm's length the past week. But honestly, it was driving him nuts. He had a good mind to march down to the paper and demand to know what was going on with the story. Like seriously, how long did it take to type up a goddamn article? Murphy sighed. He wasn't going to do anything so foolish. He just wished this whole damn thing with FF&C would come to a head so they could put it behind them and move on to other things. Like discussing the L word.

He shook his head. Nope, now was not the time, no matter how much he wished otherwise. They had to stay focused, vigilant, and keep the block safe. The cameras Joe had installed outside the front and back of Kaffeinate had to be manned, middle of the night patrols were a necessity, and they had to be constantly aware. It wasn't only bricks and mortar at stake, but people's livelihoods and lives. It seemed beyond selfish to be thinking about his own heart, his own future, when so much was at stake.

Murphy slid from the bed and strode across the cool wood floor toward the bathroom. If he was going to be wide-awake, he might as well get up and get something done. Maybe he'd take a stroll around the block before he went and got his coffee.

After a quick shower, Murphy headed down the back steps. He walked down the alley, scanning the area for anything amiss. He pulled out his penlight and checked the dark alcoves as he passed. Nothing seemed out of place, no signs of break-ins or vandalism. At the end of the alley, he stepped around the corner and pocketed his flashlight. The main streets were well lighted with lamps and colorful storefront illuminations. His timing was perfect. He stopped outside of Kaffeinate just as Joe was unlocking the door.

Joe pushed the door open and grabbed Murphy's arm, yanking him inside. "Hurry, you have to see this."

He pulled so hard, Murphy nearly lost his footing. "Whoa, what the hell, Joe?"

He ignored Murphy's protest and pulled him to the counter. "Look!"

Murphy frowned. No sight of his coffee or sweet roll, only the morning paper, and it wasn't even turned to the sports section. It surprised him how sad it made him feel. He'd gotten so used to the special treatment.

"Well?"

"Well, what?" Murphy asked in confusion.

Joe snatched up the paper and shoved it in Murphy's face. "Read the damn headline."

Tampa's Corruption Runs Deep

Astonished, Murphy met Joe's gaze. "Is this what I think it is?"

Joe smiled, showing off rows of pearly whites, and nodded. He kissed Murphy soundly, then placed the paper on the counter. "Sit down. I'll get your coffee while you read."

Excited, Murphy's legs began to shake, and he gladly did as Joe instructed. He picked up the paper and read:

TAMPA BAY—A federal grand jury on Friday handed down a sealed indictment against President and CEO Reginald Fields Sr. of Fields, Fields, and Cohen, a Tampa Bay-based resort development corporation. Fields was taken into custody over the weekend and may qualify for release after posting bail following the initial court hearing, which was not scheduled as of press time Sunday night. While most details of the now partially sealed indictment are not available, a source in the federal prosecutor's office confirmed Fields will stand trial for bribery, extortion, and conspiracy to commit murder.

The far-reaching investigation at local and state levels was launched approximately two weeks ago after evidence came to light that proves corruption on a mass scale. An anonymous tip made to the Tribune *sparked the investigation.*

John Clare, assistant to Florida Governor Douglas Walker, was also named in the indictment. The governor was unavailable for comment.

Joe set an iced coffee down in front of Murphy, and he reached for it. "So that's it." Tilting his head up, he met Joe's gaze. "We did it."

Joe leaned down and pressed a kiss to Murphy's lips. "No, you did it."

"I can't believe they've already indicted him. I've been watching the news like a hawk and there hasn't been so much as a peep."

"My guess is Mitch took it straight to the authorities. I'm not sure how they were able to keep it hush-hush, but obviously they did."

"So it's over? No more worries?" Murphy asked. He should have felt some joy, or at the very least some relief, but his stomach was still in knots for some reason he couldn't quite understand.

"Our part in it is over. I'm sure Fields isn't going to go down easy. However, now that he's been exposed for the scumbag that he is, I highly doubt he'll be messing with our little neck of the woods."

Murphy jumped up and threw his arms around Joe's neck and hugged him tight. "This calls for a celebration!"

Chapter Twenty-Five

JOE LEANED against the brick wall outside Kaffeinate, watching the evening partygoers and tourists as they passed. Everyone seemed in good spirits, adding to Joe's feel-good mood. He glanced down at his watch. He'd be a whole lot happier if Murphy would hurry up. He pulled his phone from his pocket and dialed.

Murphy answered on the second ring. "What's up, buttercup?"

"What are you doing?"

"Patience, patience."

"I don't want to be patient, I'm hungry. What's taking you so long?"

"Sorry, babe, my mom called," Murphy explained. "I'll be right down."

"Aww, that's so cute. A mommy's boy."

"Fuck you." The sting in the harsh words was eased by laughter before the line went dead.

Joe returned his phone to his pocket. He really was hungry, but he was even more anxious to take Murphy out and simply enjoy a night of fun. A dark cloud had been hanging over their heads for the past couple of weeks. Now that the sun was out—not literally, mind you, but still—he was ready to soak it up.

Tapping his foot impatiently, Joe tried to keep the irritation off his face as he nodded to the people passing by. He returned a wave, checked his watch again, and wiped sweat from his brow.

"C'mon, Murphy," he mumbled. His breath hitched when Murphy stepped around the corner. If Joe's knees hadn't gone weak, he would've rushed him. Joe licked his lips. "Well, hello, handsome."

Murphy preened, pushing out his chest, putting his arms out, and turning three-sixty, giving Joe a show. His linen pants stretched tight across his ass, and his baby blue dress shirt was tailored perfectly to show off his incredible form.

"I take it back." Joe stalked closer. "You're not just handsome, you're fucking hot."

A rosy blush colored Murphy's cheeks. "My pants are a size smaller than I normally get. I can't breathe, truth be told."

Joe snickered. "Well, I won't make you wear them any longer than absolutely necessary."

"Yeah, well, I don't think I can eat in these. I better go change." Murphy turned on his heel and started back the way he came.

Joe stood mesmerized by the gentle sway of Murphy's tight bum. It took a second for his lust-scattered brain to catch up, and he stopped Murphy before he could get too far away. "If you'll leave them on, I promise to make it worth your while later."

Murphy stared up at him for a moment, then arched a brow. "How so?"

"You wouldn't want to ruin your surprise, would you?" Joe spun Murphy around and drew him near, letting him feel Joe's growing arousal.

Murphy ground his groin against Joe for a moment, then suddenly froze. "Bad idea." He pulled from Joe's grasp and pressed his palm against his dick. "There is barely enough room for the boys as it is."

Joe had to laugh at that. "I will try to behave." He took Murphy's hand in his, bent, and kissed it. He looked up at Murphy from beneath his lashes. "For now."

"Knock it off or you'll be going without dinner," Murphy chastised. He tugged Joe's hand. "So what are you in the mood to eat?"

Joe started to open his mouth, but Murphy shushed him with a single finger. "Don't even say it."

"What?" Joe feigned innocence. "It's like you think you know what I was going to say."

"I know how your mind works. Besides, I know what *I* would have said, and seeing as you're a bigger horndog than me...." Murphy smirked. "Anyway, where are we headed?"

"I was going to suggest a great big platter of greasy deep-fried seafood and beer. However, since you're worried about your girlish figure, I know a wonderful vegan place a couple blocks over. They do amazing things with seagrass and tofu."

"You feed me grass and beans and I swear you'll go without dick for an entire month," Murphy growled lowly.

"The Shack, it is," Joe announced and turned them around to head in the opposite direction.

MURPHY SHIFTED in his seat uncomfortably. It had little to do with the large amount of fried shrimp, grouper, and scallops he'd consumed, nor the four beers he'd polished off, although his pants *were* a bit tight, just not in the good spot. Since the night Joe had told him he loved him, Murphy'd had a hard time thinking of anything else. He was still kicking himself in the ass for stopping Joe from professing his love. It had shocked Murphy to his core, and because he hadn't known how to respond, he'd avoided the whole awkward moment for fear he'd make a complete fool of himself.

"Murphy?"

The concern in Joe's voice snapped Murphy out of his musings. "I'm sorry, what were you saying?"

Joe tilted his head. "I'm glad to see you came back."

"Excuse me?"

"I called your name twice," Joe explained. "Wherever you went must not have been a very nice place."

His mouth suddenly dry, Murphy picked up his beer and took a swig. "What makes you think that?"

Joe reached across the table and ran the tip of his finger between Murphy's brows. "You still have the frown lines."

Murphy took Joe's hand and kissed his knuckles. "I just zoned out for a moment. What were you asking?"

"Only if you were ready for dessert."

Murphy downed the last of his beer. "Ready whenever you are."

Joe laughed. "And you call me a horndog."

"You are, and an insatiable one as well."

"And yet here I was talking about a slice of apple pie topped with vanilla ice cream and caramel."

Glad he'd been pulled from his wandering thoughts and into a situation he could control, Murphy stretched his foot out and ran it up and down Joe's calf. "Sure you were."

"I'm quite serious." Joe waved over the waitress, to Murphy's great shock. He would have sworn Joe would have been on his feet and pulling Murphy out of the place. He had the sneaking suspicion Joe was up to something. Murphy would just have to redouble his efforts to find out.

Kicking off his loafer, Murphy ran his foot up Joe's calf to his thigh. He teased the inside seam of Joe's pants with his toes while Joe ordered his dessert and two more beers. Murphy hid his grin behind his napkin as he wiped the remnants of grease from his lips when Joe tensed. Murphy scooched down farther in his chair and inched his foot closer.

Joe tightened his hand around Murphy's foot and tsked.

Murphy tried to push forward, but the hold on his foot tightened. "I was just trying to scratch my foot."

"Uh-huh." Joe pushed Murphy's foot off his lap. "Are you sure you don't want some dessert?"

Murphy let out an exasperated breath. He wasn't used to this side of Joe. Murphy was used to Joe practically accosting him in public, always ready for a romp.

He narrowed his eyes at the smugly smiling man. "What are you up to?"

Joe leaned back in his chair, taking his half-empty beer with him. "I'm enjoying a nice dinner with great conversation and looking forward to topping it off with a little sweet treat."

"Joe," Murphy growled.

"Murphy," Joe responded, his smile growing.

"I—"

"Oh look, here comes my pie."

Murphy was tempted to shake the man, better yet, to spank him. *That's it! Sneaky bastard is doing it on purpose.* To prove Murphy right, Joe dipped his finger in his ice cream, then sucked the entire digit into his mouth, letting out a tiny moan.

"I take it it's good?" Murphy asked.

"It's to die for. Want a bite?"

Murphy nodded, a plan forming. Two could play this game. Joe dipped his spoon into the ice cream, scooped up a bit, and offered it to Murphy. He took the bite. It was good, but not moan-worthy.

"It's okay, but maybe it's better the way you had it."

Joe dipped his finger in the cream. "Like this?"

Without taking his gaze from him, Murphy clutched his wrist and brought Joe's hand to his mouth. He gave Joe's finger much the same treatment but added a little tongue, swirling it around the digit and not even trying to be discreet when he moaned.

"Mmm, you're right, it is amazing. You going to share the rest?"

Joe shifted in his seat, and the lustful look in his eyes told Murphy that Joe was losing some of his control. "Sure, but I think maybe I should have another spoon brought over."

"No need." Murphy picked up a section of apple. He lapped at it with the tip of his tongue, then sealed his lips around it and slowly sucked it into his mouth. He was rewarded with a deep rumbling moan from Joe. *Gotcha.*

Joe growled and gestured toward the waitress. "Check."

Murphy couldn't help but laugh.

"Yuck it up. You'll be paying for your teasing later."

Murphy picked up another apple and popped it into his mouth. "Right after I spank your ass for trying to do it to me."

"Check!" Joe called out again, causing Murphy to laugh even harder.

As soon as Joe paid the bill, Murphy had to practically run to keep up with Joe's long stride as he hurried out of the Seafood Shack.

"My place or yours?"

"They're both your places," Murphy reminded him. "You pick."

"Not arguing that point at this moment. Beach house is closer."

At least things were back to normal: no arguing, no deep conversation, just raw animalistic lust surging between them. Hands roaming, clothes disappearing before they even made it inside Joe's house.

Once they crossed the threshold, Joe pulled Murphy into his arms, pushed him against the wall, and sealed their lips together.

Murphy opened his mouth, welcoming his lover's tongue inside. God, it was good. Each time their lips met, sparks ignited, sending a tingling sensation to race across every nerve ending in Murphy's body. He'd never had a lover who could consume him so completely with a simple touch, a soft kiss. Never had anyone he couldn't get enough of. However, there was that little business about a bit of payback. A tease who needed to learn a lesson.

Ending the kiss, Murphy spun them until Joe's back was pinned against the door. He sucked up a mark on the side of Joe's neck, then moved down Joe's chest, stopping long enough to give each nipple some attention until they were hard and Joe was moaning and arching into the touch. Murphy licked, nipped, and kissed toward Joe's navel. He teased it with his tongue while he dipped his finger beneath the waistband of Joe's pants.

"Mmm, I like the way you think, baby," Joe groaned, thrusting his hips out. Rather than going to his knees, Murphy moved back up Joe's body. "Hey, I liked you down there," Joe grumbled.

"I know you did." He cupped Joe's dick in the palm of his hand and squeezed slightly. "But if I recall, you're due a little punishment."

Joe grabbed Murphy's hips and pulled him close. "Aww, c'mon, baby, don't you want to take the edge off first?"

The heat in Joe's eyes was enough to set Murphy's blood to run hot and his dick to throb. "Oh, one of us will be on the edge soon enough." He pulled out of Joe's grasp. "Now get your fine ass in the bedroom." A visible shudder ripped through Joe, and Murphy couldn't help but feel a bit cocky.

Murphy followed Joe into the bedroom. "Strip the rest of those clothes off."

Without taking his gaze from Joe as he shucked his pants and briefs, Murphy unfastened his belt and slacks and shoved them down, wincing when the tight linen pressed against his hard cock. He pushed them down his thighs and then let them fall down his calves and kicked out of them.

Joe stood gloriously naked, hands on his hips. "What now?"

Murphy stepped up close, took Joe's flushed and leaking cock in a loose grip, and stroked it from base to tip. He went up on tiptoe and brushed his lips against Joe's. "Now I get to show you why you should never try to out-tease the master. Get on the bed. Hands and knees."

Joe let out an honest-to-God whine and stepped back when Murphy released the hold he had on his cock. Murphy bit down on his bottom lip to keep from laughing at the pitiful sound. Still, Joe did as he was told. He climbed up on the bed and started to move toward the center.

Murphy grabbed his calf. "Stop there. Feet hanging over the edge of the mattress, knees spread."

Joe got into position, that sweet, tight ass swaying with each movement. Murphy couldn't resist such temptation. He drew back and landed a slap on Joe's right buttcheek.

"Ohh, baby, do it again," Joe taunted.

"That wasn't for you. That was for me."

Murphy buried his face in Joe's ass, licking and lapping at the sweet little hole. Joe groaned deep and needy, his back arching. While he continued to rim Joe, Murphy reached around and took Joe's hard cock in his hand, stroking it in long firm pulls. It took no time at all before Joe was squirming, thigh muscles shaking, moans and pleas pouring from him, and Murphy quickened the pace of his hand while stabbing his tongue in and out of Joe's ass at the same pace.

The trembling in Joe's legs increased as did the sounds pouring from him. Murphy could tell from Joe's movements and the way his dick pulsed against Murphy's hand that he was close. Murphy released his hold on Joe's dick, straightened, and rested his hand on Joe's hip to steady himself. Joe wasn't the only one who was shaking.

"What the hell, Murphy? Why did you quit?"

"I was thinking maybe we should take a nice long stroll on the beach. The moon is full. It would be quite romantic."

Joe's brows shot up to his hairline briefly, and then he narrowed his eyes. "This is what you meant by payback, isn't it?"

Murphy smiled broadly. "I'm sure I have no idea what you're talking about."

Joe moved so quickly Murphy didn't have time to respond: the next thing he knew he was lying on his back on the mattress with Joe staring down at him. "If I promise to never do it again, will you forgive me for teasing you and fuck me?"

Murphy pretended to consider it for a moment, but with the look of lust in Joe's eyes and the hard cock pressing against his thigh, there really was only one answer. He threaded his fingers in Joe's hair, pulled his face down, and took his mouth in a blistering kiss.

WITHOUT BREAKING the kiss, Joe struggled to find the lube he'd tucked away under his pillow as Murphy continued to attack his mouth. After a moment of fumbling, he managed to not only find it, but open it as well. *Yay, me*. It didn't matter that he got as much of the stuff on the bed as he did on his hand, or that the bottle wasn't quite closed when he dropped it beside him on the mattress.

Joe sat back and held Murphy's gaze. "Let me make it up to you, baby," he cooed, then reached around to lube up his ass.

"Damn, Joe."

Joe plunged his fingers as deep as he could into his ass, moaning while he twisted and scissored to stretch the tight muscles. He gasped and arched when Murphy wrapped his fist around Joe's cock and pumped it hard and fast.

"Fuck. Murphy! Condom. Under," Joe said tightly, pointing with his free hand toward the pillow.

Blessedly, Murphy released Joe's dick just in time. A knot was forming at the base of Joe's spine and it wouldn't take much. "Got that thing on yet?"

"Give me a second, will you. You're not anxious or anything, are you?" Murphy tossed back. He threw the wrapper aside and rolled the condom down his length.

Joe couldn't have responded right then if his life had depended on it. He pulled his fingers free and grasped Murphy's sheathed cock, spreading the lube over it. Joe straddled Murphy's body, lined up over Murphy's dick, and impaled himself on it in one swift movement, pulling a strangled cry from Murphy.

For several long moments, they both held still, breathing hard. Jolts of electricity raced down Joe's back. The pleasure was so intense he could scarcely breathe. Joe's body craved release, but he fought it with every fiber of his being. Murphy filled and stretched him so completely, and Joe could feel Murphy's cock pulsing deep within him. He planted his hands on Murphy's broad chest and panted until the urge to come eased.

"You nearly made me come," Murphy gritted out.

"That makes two of us." Joe leaned down and took Murphy's mouth in a slow lazy kiss. They breathed each other in, giving them both a chance to calm slightly. Joe sure as hell needed it, or he'd be coming after the first thrust.

After what seemed an eternity, the urgency in Joe passed. The tension in Murphy's chest eased, signaling he was in better control, and Joe rocked his hips.

Murphy gasped. "Love the way your ass feels around me."

Joe moved again, another slow roll of his hips against Murphy's body. "And the way you fill me…. God, Murphy…. So good."

Joe sat back, planting his hands on Murphy's thighs. Murphy grasped Joe's hips, and together they moved in perfect sync. Joe knew it wouldn't last long, it couldn't. The night of teasing, the thick cock inside him, the blunt fingers digging into his hips were conspiring against his restraint.

Murphy let out a ragged moan. One hand found Joe's dick and wrapped around it with just the right amount of pressure, creating a delicious amount of friction. "That's it, baby."

Joe stared, in awe of the man he was straddling. God, he loved seeing Murphy like this, his face flushed and his eyes filled with desire. Digging his fingers into Murphy's taut thighs, Joe rose till only the head of Murphy's cock breached him. Then, painfully slow, he lowered himself again. Over and over he repeated the movement until he pulled a strangled sound from Murphy.

The intensity increased exponentially. Every nerve ending in Joe's body tingled with desire, building, climbing with each movement. Murphy's cock swelled impossibly thicker, stretching Joe's ass, magnifying each movement into an explosion of sensation. Murphy stroked Joe's cock in time with their mutual thrusts, creating a soundtrack of moans and sighs from Joe.

From the way Murphy was shaking and arching, he wasn't going to last, but that was okay since Joe was already teetering on the edge himself.

Suddenly he was no longer just teetering but falling headfirst into pleasure, and he barely had time to grit out, "Coming," before the first drops of his release landed on Murphy's stomach.

"Come on, baby, give it to me." He tightened his grip on Joe's cock and pumped hard and fast, demanding every drop.

Whimpering, Joe lifted up and slammed himself down one last time, driving Murphy's cock in as deep as it would go. Murphy nearly bucked him off when he arched and shouted out Joe's name as he came deep within Joe's ass.

Joe fell forward onto Murphy's chest, panting, breathing in Murphy's scent. He groaned when Murphy slipped from his body, then nuzzled in. "Damn, baby. I really, really needed that."

"Mmm hmmm. Me too." Murphy wrapped his arms around Joe, holding him tight while the fingers of one hand drew random patterns along Joe's spine. "I'm glad we decided to come here. Your bed is so much more comfortable than mine."

"You know, you could sleep in this bed every night," Joe said hesitantly. Murphy's hand stuttered along Joe's skin.

Joe swallowed but didn't regret saying it. It had been on the tip of his tongue ever since he'd professed his love for Murphy. However, he'd known not to bring it up again while the shit with FF&C was unsettled. Now that it appeared the company would be too busy with bigger problems, Joe figured they'd have little time to worry about Joe's little slice of Tampa. Besides, he loved Murphy, wanted to spend a lifetime with him. If he was going to share his heart, it was only natural that he'd want to share his home as well.

"Joe—"

Joe lifted up and met Murphy's gaze. "Say you'll live with me." Joe laid a hand on Murphy's chest directly over his heart. "I promised I wouldn't bring it up until the mess with FF&C was over, and I kept that promise. But dammit, Murphy, I love you and I don't want to spend another night without you next to me. I don't ever want to wake up without you next to me." He pressed a soft kiss to Murphy's lips. "Please say you'll stay?"

"I don't know, I kind of like living at the apartment." A playful smile curled the edge of Murphy's lips. "It's close to my favorite coffee place."

"Sorry, it's not available."

"Oh?"

"Nope. I promised it to Kallie."

Murphy arched a brow at him. "Seriously?"

Joe couldn't hold back his smile. "No, but I'm sure she'd be interested. Maybe she and Jeremy could rent it together."

"I'd be careful playing matchmaker for Kallie. I have a feeling she won't stand for it, and you know you can't afford to lose her," Murphy pointed out.

"I know that. I'm not trying to hook them up. From what I saw when I stepped out of my office the other day, I don't have to."

"Oh really?"

"Yup, but I don't want to talk about them. Whether they rent it or not is irrelevant. You did such an amazing job, I'm sure I'll be able to find a tenant at top dollar in no time." He laid his palm against Murphy's jaw. "So, what do you say? Will you live with me?"

Murphy worried his lower lip between his teeth. "Wow. Damn. Are you sure this is what you want? I can be bossy."

"Oh, don't I know it." Joe grinned. "But I'm willing to let you boss me around once in a while, if you promise to keep me in line with a good swat on the ass from time to time."

"You liked that, did you," Murphy asked knowingly.

"You know I did. Then again, I love all the things you do to me. So say you'll live with me. Please?"

Murphy stared at him for a brief tense moment. Joe held his breath, hoping and silently willing Murphy to say yes. When a broad smile spread across Murphy's face, Joe let out the breath, and warmth spread through him.

"Okay."

"You'll live with me?"

"Yeah. You may end up regretting it. I'm a bit of a bed hog and I don't cuddle, ya know."

"Yes, Murphy, I know, and I seriously doubt I'll regret how little you cuddle." Joe chuckled. "Shall we seal it with a kiss?"

Murphy grabbed Joe's face in both hands and brought their mouths together. It was gentle, unhurried, full of the promise they were making to each other. To Joe, nothing had ever felt so right. It wouldn't always be easy, considering how passionate they both were, and how quick to growl. However, with the way Murphy came in and stole Joe's heart, he was willing to learn to work on his quick temper. Because life without Murphy didn't seem like much of a life, at least not a happy one.

Murphy ended the kiss, brushing his lips along Joe's jaw. "It's not going to be easy, ya know? I'm difficult to deal with at times. Some may even say I'm a bit stubborn."

Joe arched a brow. "A *bit* stubborn?"

"Don't even be calling me out on that, mister. You've got quite the stubborn streak too."

"Just more proof we're perfect for each other," Joe pointed out happily.

"No, we'd be perfect together if we weren't stuck together with sloppy bodily fluids." Murphy yawned, big. "I'm exhausted, babe."

Joe kissed Murphy's nose, then slid off him. "Well, then, let's get my man cleaned up and tucked in bed."

"I'll wash your back if you'll wash mine?" Murphy offered.

Joe's chest tightened pleasantly as it hit him. Murphy would be in his bed every night, and washing each other's back would be a daily occurrence. Damn, he was a lucky man. He left the bed and held his hand out for Murphy. As soon as Murphy was on his feet, Joe pulled him in for another slow and sweet kiss, then, smiling, Joe entwined their fingers and led Murphy to the shower. *Our shower*. His smile grew even larger.

Epilogue

STANDING ON the back deck, Joe stared out over the ocean. He took in a deep breath, the scent of salt and brine on the early evening breeze. Over the past couple of weeks, he and Murphy had worked side by side in the evenings to build the deck. It was now one of Joe's favorite spots to hang out after work. Although they both had tempers with short fuses, they discovered they worked exceptionally well together. That is, as long as they agreed on something. When they didn't.... Joe laughed and shook his head when he remembered the spat they'd had over the railing. He'd wanted traditional wood spindles, Murphy insisting metal and glass would give an unobstructed view of the beach. Joe had lost the bet, coming seconds before Murphy did. They settled most disputes with competitive sex, which in Joe's opinion was the only way to do it. A win-win situation. He ran his hand along the warm metal and smiled. He'd lost the bet but certainly didn't feel like a loser. He'd gotten a mind-blowing orgasm, and the new glass railing was stunning.

"Your screw mimosa, sir," Murphy announced.

Joe accepted the drink and slid his arm around Murphy's waist. "Another thing you were right about." Adding vodka to a simple mimosa was pure brilliance and delicious too.

"Am I ever wrong?"

"Well...."

Laughing, Murphy bumped Joe's thigh. "Don't answer that. But what was the other thing I was right about?"

"I was admiring the railing." He steered Murphy back toward the double lounge chair. Joe set his drink on the table and pulled Murphy down onto the cushions. "I love the view from here."

"Told you so," Murphy responded with a cocky smile. "You really should listen to me more often."

"What? I listen to you all the time."

Murphy shifted up closer to Joe and threw his leg over Joe's thighs, then nuzzled the side of his neck. "Not true. If you had, we'd be shucking some clothes and banging with this gorgeous view as a backdrop rather than having to entertain people."

A shudder went through Joe when Murphy flicked his tongue over a sensitive spot below Joe's ear. Heat pooled in his groin, hardening his cock. Damn, why did he have to invite Kallie and Jeremy over? He tended to be happiest when it was just him and Murphy, but he could see where it would be easy to become a hermit. The last thing he wanted to do was alienate his friends.

Sighing dramatically, he shoved Murphy's leg off his lap and pressed his palm to his dick. "You can make me pay for my lapse in good judgment later. How's dinner coming along?" Joe asked, needing a change of topic before he ravaged Murphy right there and then.

"Everything is ready. All you have to do is fire up the grill when they get here."

Joe leaned over and pressed a chaste kiss to Murphy's cheek. "What would I do without you?" Murphy turned his head and tried to capture Joe's lips, but Joe anticipated the movement and rolled out of the way.

Murphy frowned. "I was going to say be a lot less satisfied, but that may be in your very near future. Now get back over here and kiss me."

"Is that the doorbell I hear?"

Murphy's frown deepened, but before he could call Joe out on his little white lie, the doorbell did ring.

"I'll get it."

"Uh-huh," Murphy huffed.

Joe made his way to the front door and couldn't help but smile. He loved the fact that Murphy couldn't keep his hands off him and was proving to be just as insatiable sexually as he was. They really were very well matched.

Joe opened the door to find Kallie standing there with a wide smile and a plate of sweet rolls. "Hi! I brought dessert," she announced and thrust the plate at Joe.

"You shouldn't have." He stared down at the same rolls he saw every morning. "Really, you shouldn't have."

"I didn't. Mrs. Williams did." Kallie pushed past him, tugging Jeremy along with her. Jeremy's cheeks turned pink, but he looked happier than Joe had ever seen him.

"Murphy's out on the deck. Why don't you join him and I'll get you something to drink."

"Thanks, I'll have a beer," Kallie called out.

"I'll have the same," Jeremy said.

Joe set the rolls on the kitchen counter, then grabbed drinks for their guests before joining them.

"Oh. My. God. Joe, this deck looks amazing," Kallie commented, accepting the beer. "I am so jealous. You must love spending your evenings out here."

Murphy waggled his brows. "Some evenings more than others."

Kallie slapped Murphy's arm. "Keep it in your pants. You have company," she teased. "But seriously, this is stunning."

"Thanks. Murphy is an amazing handyman." Joe picked up his drink from the table and held it up, toasting Murphy.

Murphy preened a little at the compliment.

"You don't have to tell me. I saw what he did with the apartment. Speaking of which. Have you listed it yet?"

"Not yet. I haven't had time to set up the ad. Why do you ask?"

"I was thinking, maybe I...." She turned her head toward Jeremy. "Or rather, we, could rent it."

Joe snorted and nearly choked on his drink. Murphy joined him in laughter.

Kallie narrowed her eyes, one dainty hand on her hip. "What the hell is so damn funny?"

Joe met Murphy's gaze, which was a bad idea because it caused him to laugh even harder.

Kallie didn't look impressed. "Whatever, Joe. If you don't want to rent it to us, just say so."

Joe stepped up close to her and draped his arm over her shoulder. "Sorry, I wasn't laughing at you. Of course you can rent it." She gazed at him with a wary expression, and Joe squeezed her tighter. "Seriously, I can't think of anyone I'd rather see living there."

That settled, the topic turned to idle chitchat about work, renovations, the weather—light things while Murphy wielded the spatula. The delicious aroma of grilled chicken and smoked applewood caused Joe's stomach to growl. He had easily fallen into the role of preparing their evening meals unless they were cooking outdoors, then Murphy took on the job with relish. He was damn good at it too.

With full bellies, the four of them sat with after-dinner drinks, enjoying the cool breeze. It was an unseasonably warm autumn, so Joe's favorite time was quickly becoming the cooler evenings he could sit outside and snuggle with Murphy beneath a light blanket.

"So, you and Jeremy, huh?" Murphy hummed.

"So, you and Joe, huh?" Kallie countered.

"Damn, there has been a lot brewing at Joe's, and I ain't talking coffee," Jeremy added.

They all stared for a moment at the man who rarely said much and then burst out laughing. Joe snuggled into Murphy's side and kissed his cheek. So much more than coffee *had* been brewing, and Joe was one damn lucky man.

SJD PETERSON, better known as Jo, is a best-selling and award-winning author of gay romance. She lives in Michigan with her Itty Bitty Kitty and Little Man. She does her best writing when under pressure of deadlines and at 3:00 a.m. when the world is quiet. Jo loves to tell stories about real people with real flaws. The happily-ever-after isn't guaranteed unless it's earned through hard work and growth. Oh, but when it comes, the rewards are all the better!

Facebook: www.facebook.com/SJD.Peterson
Blog: sjdpeterson.blogspot.com
Twitter: @SJDPeterson
Goodreads: www.goodreads.com/author/show/4563849.S_J_D_
Peterson
Email: sjdpeterson@gmail.com

With his fauxhawk, sleeve tattoos, and visible piercings, Ridley Corbin has the whole badass vibe going on in spades. The image serves him well as the self-proclaimed protector of the underdog, and he wants nothing more than to be Alex Firestone's hero.

Alex, a mild-mannered library assistant, has moved to Slater, a quiet college town, hoping to hide from his past. He keeps to himself, but that doesn't save him from catching the unwanted attention of the campus bully. But not all is as it seems. Alex's past comes calling, and it's time he becomes top dog.

www.dreamspinnerpress.com

CAN DESTINY
AWAKEN A COLD,
DEAD HEART?

IUNCTIŌ CŌPULA

INNOCENCE
TO THE
MAX

SJD PETERSON

On his sixteenth birthday, Francisco "Cisco" Aguilar first sets eyes on Maximilian De Ferrari, owner of Wicked Grounds, an exclusive BDSM club. Cisco has been lost, unsure of what is missing in his life. Over a century old, Max leads a vampire clan, and Cisco is drawn to him in a way he can't explain. The moment he sees Max he knows his quest isn't about what he's been missing, but who.

Five years' wait seems more than Cisco can bear, but he perseveres and on his twenty-first birthday he walks into Wicked Ground. He's unafraid to meet the vampire he's sure is his destiny. Max has been waiting for him, too.

What Max has known all these years, and what Cisco soon discovers, is that more than fate is drawing them together. Iunctio Copula is a powerful binding link capable of restoring cold, dead hearts. With Max and Cisco bound, Cisco will be Max's greatest weakness. Unable to let Max go, Cisco is thrust into a dark world, where he's nearly powerless, left to fight for his life and his future with Max. Worse, he's at the mercy of those who will use him—and hurt him—just to get to the powerful vampire.

www.dreamspinnerpress.com

MY
HOMETOWN

SJD Peterson

Jimmy Brink and Eric Halter grew up together in a small country town. While Eric has always been content with life as a rancher, Jimmy wanted more and moved to Chicago early on to pursue a medical career.

Life has a way of coming back around. When Jimmy's parents decide to retire in Florida, Jimmy returns to his hometown to finish his residency at a local hospital. Flamboyant boyfriend Oliver in tow, Jimmy bumps into his old friend. Eric quickly takes a disliking to Oliver, though, and for good reason. Oliver proves he's not only self-centered but also a cheater.

To complicate matters, Eric finds it more and more difficult to hide his attraction to his best friend. When the opportunity arises, he needs to decide whether to risk their friendship to pursue his feelings… but maybe Jimmy will see there's more for him now than ever before in his hometown.

www.dreamspinnerpress.com

Officer Thomas Webber made a vow of marriage to his wife, a vow to his God to resist temptation, and a vow to uphold the law. But when Tom is forced to shelter a dark-haired stranger from the tornado raging over the county, long suppressed desires are brought to the surface and he is powerless to resist.

Ben Parker has hidden his true nature his whole life. The laws in 1952 are very clear, and to expose himself would mean rotting in jail, shunned or worse, a possible death sentence. Unable to find a job, he turned to crime. Seven years later, he's still angry and tired of hiding who he really is from the world. After meeting Thomas, Ben can envision himself settling down for the first time. The only problem is, he's already forced Thomas to break the law and become his alibi. And then there's the little obstacle of Tom's wife, family, and commitment to the town of Ramer.

Ben knows what he wants, but in order to get it, Tom will have to turn his back on society and the vows he's made if they are to find the happiness they deserve.

www.dreamspinnerpress.com

S.A. McAuley
SJD Peterson

RUIN PORN

There is underlying beauty in destruction....

Miah Thade, Finn Reese, and Ritchie Meyer are Resonator, an indie rock band with an edge—best friends turned rock stars, known as the Detroit 3. When Evin Rene appears in their life, none of them can deny he belongs with Rez.

They may have named their first album Ruin Porn because people get off on seeing how Detroit went from deeply loved to thoroughly forsaken, but they're determined to prove that blight isn't the entire story and blight isn't always ugly.

Ritchie, Miah, Finn, and Evin take Resonator to a level no one anticipates. But no prosperity comes without sacrifice, and no secret stays hidden without a trail of lies. As Rez's fame grows, so does the intensity between two of its members… as well as their potential for destruction.

Evin and Finn are about to discover the underlying beauty in their ruin porn.

www.dreamspinnerpress.com

OVERRIDE

SJD PETERSON

An Underground Club Tale

Don't judge a book by its cover....

At over six feet, with a body honed in the gym, auto worker Donavan Gregory is used to people assuming he's a dominant top. Unfortunately, they're wrong, and Donavan's desire to explore his submissive side goes unfulfilled.

Smaller and older than Donavan, Dr. Seth Manning might not look like a typical Dominant, but when the two men meet at Pride, Donavan realizes Seth might be his perfect counterpart. The trouble is, Donavan doesn't have as much experience with the BDSM world as he'd like. What could an educated, handsome, and confident man like Seth possibly see in someone like him? Seth must convince him that despite the differences on the surface, when it comes to kinky fun and discovery, they'll fit together just fine.

www.dreamspinnerpress.com

LIMITLESS
SJD PETERSON

An Underground Club Tale

Even within the context of the Underground BDSM Club, Joshua's desires are dark and extreme. Hopelessly addicted to pain and the high it gives him, he has no limits. Joshua would quite literally rather die than use a safeword, and he accepts that might be his fate. As much as he depends on others, he has yet to find a man who can gain his trust, and he has little hope that he ever will.

For Nash, acquiring Joshua from another Dom at the club is only the first step in what will be a long and arduous road to lure the young man back from the brink of self-destruction. He must do the impossible and win Joshua's trust, and he must be the one to set limits in their exploration—something he's unaccustomed to as a Dom. But Nash knows dominance doesn't always mean pushing a submissive's boundaries. It's about establishing a bond and fulfilling another man's needs. In Joshua's case, he'll have to strike a balance between meeting the young man's expectations and drawing firm lines that will save Joshua from himself.

www.dreamspinnerpress.com

www.ingramcontent.com/pod-product-compliance
Lightning Source LLC
Chambersburg PA
CBHW060102260626
47160CB00005B/1760